S0-AIE-070

9-10-99
14.95

CLINTON-MACOMB PUBLIC LIBRARY
SOUTH

NORTH TO IRON COUNTRY

A Dream-Quest Adventure

Janie Lynn Panagopoulos

River Road Publications, Inc.

ISBN: 0-938682-48-2
Printed in the United States of America

Copyright © 1996 by Janie Lynn Panagopoulos

All rights reserved. No part of this book may be reproduced or utilized in any form or by any means, electronic or mechanical, including photocopying, recording, or by an information storage and retrieval system without permission in writing from the publisher. Inquiries should be sent to River Road Publications, Inc., 830 East Savidge Street, Spring Lake, Michigan 49456-1961.

Lake Superior

Vermilion Range

Mesabi Range

Gogebic Range

Michigan

Marquette

Menominee Range   Marquette Range

Saulte

Mackina

Minnesota
Territory

Wisconsin

Green Bay

Michigan

Lake
Michigan

North
to Iron
Country

Contents

Special Thanks

A special thanks to my friends and family that supported and encouraged me as I worked on this project.

I want to especially thank those whose names, either first or last, are included in this book. The characters in the story are fictional, however, and in no way resemble real people.

A special thanks to: Dorothy Runyon, Robert Chambers, James Pacquette, Mary Margaret Chambers, Margaret Peschel, Tom Friggens, James Meyerle, James Blount, Kenn Kuester, Dave Whitaker, Dennis Panagopoulos, "Frenchy" Jean Yargeau, Jack Larson, Mike George, Shane Clark, Karen Scott, Mark Chambers, Marilynn Knowles, Jodi Chamers and Osawa Anang.

I also want to thank the staffs at the following institutions that helped me with my research: Michigan Iron Industry Museum, Cornish Pump & Mining Museum, Wisconsin Historical Society, Forsyth Township Historical Museum, Archives of the Upper Peninsula and Northern Michigan University, Marquette County Historical Society & Museum, Fayette Historical Townsite, Iron Mountain Iron Mine and Museum, Sault St. Marie Historical Society & Museum, and Marquette Maritime Museum.

A special thanks to Linda Panian at Marquette County Historical, J.M. Longyear Research Library, and to Dean and Cheryl Cheadle of Tun-Dra Outfitters for their recommendations and information concerning dog sledding. Finally, I do not want to forget my friends at the Bellaire Public Library; Nadine Sturdy, Jean Thornell, and Linda Offenbecker.

Dedicated to the memory of my father,
Clyde Louis Blount, 1920-1982

"Have you heard this old saying about pasties?" Mrs. Runyon asked. " 'The Cornish brought them, the Norwegians made them, and the Italians perfected them.' "

Around the classroom students laughed in agreement. The Italians of Marquette were well-known for preparing good food.

"Now I'm going to draw something on the board that you all have seen," Mrs. Runyon said. "Let's see who can name it first."

She turned to the board. Now was Robert's chance. Mary had her hand halfway up already, so she could be the one to identify the drawing. Robert squinted and took careful aim at the back of her head, just above her barrette. *TWONG!*

At the same instant, Mary turned to size up her competition — and the heavy rubber band stung her smartly on the tip of the nose. In pain and surprise, she let out a yelp.

Mrs. Runyon, turning from her drawing of a mining platform, demanded to know the cause of the outburst.

Her eyes filling with tears, Mary pointed at Robert and blurted, "Bobby shot me with a rubber band! He hit me in the nose!"

Except for her sobs, the class was silent. Robert was in big trouble. Mrs. Runyon came down the aisle to examine Mary's nose, which now had a small red welt.

"Robert, did you do this?"

Hanging his head, Robert nodded to admit his guilt. Without looking up, he tried to explain. "I didn't mean to hit her in the face. I was aiming for her barrette. Anyway, she always makes fun of me. She calls me 'Bobby Pack-Rat.' "

In fury, Mary yelled, "He IS a pack-rat, you should see his locker!"

Pain forgotten, she began chanting: "Bobby Pacquette's a pack-rat, Bobby Pacquette's a pack-rat, Bobby — "

"My name is Robert, not Bobby," he interrupted loudly. "Robert, like my father's name."

"All right, you two!" Mrs. Runyon said sharply.

But the next words were already flying from Mary's mouth: "Your father's dead!"

That was it. Robert quickly stood. Taller than most of the kids in his class, he was eye-to-eye with Mrs. Runyon as he tried to push past her and get to

Mary. But Mrs. Runyon grabbed Robert's arm and firmly turned him back to his seat.

"Robert Pacquette, you will sit down — now! Do you have any more rubber bands?"

Robert shook his head.

"Good. Sit down! You're staying after school. I want to talk to you. And Mary, I want you to stop teasing Robert. Do you understand me, young lady?"

Mary looked up as if to argue but then simply nodded.

Robert brooded for the rest of the school day, wondering how bad this was going to be. He couldn't stay long after school, because then he'd miss the bus. It was February and too cold to walk home.

The longer the day's lessons dragged on, the more miserable Robert felt. Finally the school secretary's voice came over the loudspeaker, dismissing the students with a reminder to dress warmly the next day — and, if the weather continued to worsen, to watch the news for the possible announcement of a "snow day."

The class cheered in the hope that school would be canceled. Even Robert's spirits lifted a bit; he could use a day off from battling with Mary.

When the announcements were finished, the bell sounded and everyone but Robert dashed for the door. Mary turned as she was leaving to give him a satisfied, smart-aleck grin.

Mrs. Runyon cleaned the board and tidied her desk until the room was cleared, then summoned Robert to stand in front of her.

"You ride the bus, don't you?"

He nodded.

"I won't keep you long," she said. "I understand how hard it has been for you since you lost your father last summer. I've been trying to help you as much as I can. I've given you chances to make up work and retake tests, but I cannot allow you to hurt other students. That's not right, and you know it."

Robert swallowed hard. Mrs. Runyon was a good teacher, and he really liked her.

"Robert, I've decided that maybe you don't have enough work to keep your mind off your troubles. I want you to do an assignment that will take some time to complete. And I am even going to give you a choice."

Robert studied his boots. Anything but more schoolwork, he thought.

"I want you to read some chapters from this book and write a report on them," Mrs. Runyon said.

From her desk the teacher took a large book called *The Honorable Peter White: A Biographical Sketch of the Lake Superior Iron Country.*

"The project should take you about two weeks," she said.

Robert felt sick. Two weeks of work? The reading alone could take him a whole *year.*

"Or, you can interview someone who has worked in the mines and write a report on their experiences. The choice is yours; either way, I want a five-page report on my desk in two weeks."

"Five pages?"

"Five. I don't think that is too much. And the next time you go to hurt someone, maybe you'll think twice.

"The choice is yours. And you'd better be quick; walking home is no fun in this weather."

Robert glanced out the window and saw snow blowing around the trees and buildings. It was too far to walk, and too cold. And the reading assignment was just too long.

"I'll interview a miner," he said sadly.

"Good. I was hoping you would choose that one. In the next year or two you will be doing **oral history** reports anyway, so this will help you prepare.

"In this folder you will find some interview sheets and information on how to take notes and write up your material. Now you'd better hurry and catch your bus. I have a couple of calls to make before I leave."

Robert hurried to his locker and then to the bus, hoping one of Mrs. Runyon's calls wouldn't be to his mother.

Chapter 2

Busted

Hanging up the phone, Margaret Pacquette allowed herself a quick grin as she watched the blowing snow outside the living-room window. She knew what she had done would not sit well with Robert. But maybe the old man could help him.

Swirling the remaining hot chocolate in her mug, she wished once again that Robert could get over his angry feelings about his father's death. If he just could accept the way things were going to be from now on . . . .

Outside, the return of the school bus was announced with a rumbling crunch of the hard-packed snow covering the road. Margaret went into the kitchen to fill a small basket with her freshly baked muffins.

Robert, dragging his backpack in the snow, slowly made his way toward the back door. Snow was still falling, and the cold was biting. Now if only the wind would get worse, he thought, there'll be too many snowdrifts to have school tomorrow.

Thor, the family's big old husky, heard him coming around the house and began tugging at the chain that tied him to the doghouse. Robert was home!

Robert dropped his pack as the dog jumped to greet him, resting its heavy paws on his shoulders. Thor licked Robert's face and investigated his jacket pockets.

"Hey, I don't have any treats for you," Robert said, roughing up the big dog's fur. Thor was a good dog; the best.

After a few minutes of play, Robert retrieved his pack and headed for the door. As soon as he opened it, he knew his mother had been baking. Great!

On the kitchen counter lay rows of chocolate-chip cookies on wax paper, muffins cooling all topsy-turvy, two loaves of fresh bread, and a small basket covered by a napkin. Robert's mother worked at the bakery downtown, but still managed to bake at home. Coming home to these smells from her kitchen always made Robert smile.

"Hi!" said his mother. "Before you get unbundled, please bring in a sling of firewood. It's been hard to keep the house warm today.

"And make sure Thor has water and food. Mr. Friggens says Thor has been ignored since your father died. He says we should still treat him like the champion **sled dog** he once was."

Robert frowned at the words of their neighbor. "Mr. Friggens doesn't know what he's talking about," Robert said. "Thor gets plenty of attention."

"I know, but just make sure, OK?"

Back outside, Robert broke the ice covering Thor's water pan and checked the big bowl of dry food. Maybe Thor should come inside tonight, even though his heavy coat was made for this kind of weather.

He played with the dog again before filling the sling from the woodpile and carrying it into the house.

"How did school go today?" his mother asked.

"It was fine," Robert replied as he took off his jacket and hung it up. He unlaced his boots and stepped out of them before crossing to the living room with the firewood.

"No, Robert. Let me ask again: how was school today?"

Busted. So Mrs. Runyon did call. I don't believe it, thought Robert. Swinging open the cast-iron door of the wood stove, he angrily tossed two pieces of wood onto the embers glowing inside, sending a flurry of sparks up the chimney.

"Robert, please be careful. Fire is nothing to play with."

In the kitchen, his mother poured hot chocolate into their mugs, topping Robert's with small marshmallows.

"It was Mary again," he said. "She's such a jerk! She acts like she's perfect, and she's always giving me a hard time. She still calls me Bobby — can you believe that?"

"So you hit her in the face with a rubber band? I don't think that's a good solution to a problem, do you?"

"I wasn't trying to hit her in the face," he explained. "She just turned. It was an accident — actually, it was her fault."

"Her fault? No. And this was no accident. Look, Robert, there are lots of people in this world. You won't always get along with all of them, but that doesn't give you the right to be mean or hurt them.

"Do you think, if your father were alive, he would be proud of you for hurting that girl, even if she made you angry?"

Trying to avoid his mother's eyes, Robert focused on the shelves lining the wall across from him. On them were at least a dozen of the wooden hawk figures his father had worked so hard at carving during his long illness. Robert knew he would not be pleased with what he had done.

"Look, Robert. I know these last months have been hard on you," his mother continued. "It's been hard on me, too. Mrs. Runyon is a fine teacher, and she's only trying to help you. You really need to start trying harder; do you understand?"

Fighting back tears, Robert faced his mother and nodded.

"Now, Mrs. Runyon told me she was giving you some extra work, an assignment that you chose?"

"I have to collect mining stories from someone that worked in the mines. I've got to talk with somebody, ask 'em questions about what it was like to work there and junk like that."

"That's good; you'll learn more about what your father's life was like."

"Yeah, maybe about how the dust in the mine killed him!" Robert exploded.

"We don't know that; the doctors said it was cancer," his mother replied calmly. "But why did you pick this assignment, if you dislike it so?"

"It was either that or read this big old monster book a zillion pages long. She gave me two weeks for this, and I have to write a report, too."

"Well, I want you to do a good job."

As Robert worked at scooping marshmallows from his mug with a chocolate-chip cookie, they heard the scraping sounds of a snow shovel on concrete. Long spaces of time elapsed between scrapes.

"That must be Mr. Friggens," Margaret said, getting up to look out the kitchen window. Robert swallowed the last of his hot chocolate with a slurp of melted marshmallow.

"I want you to take this basket of muffins to him."

"Mom? Why do I have to? He doesn't even like me. Especially after he said those things about Thor."

"Why do you have to? Because I asked you to, and because it would be nice of you. Mr. Friggens is a lonely old man, and he has been a good neighbor for years."

Robert went to the door and began getting back into his boots, jacket, stocking cap and mittens.

"You know, it would be nice if you offered to shovel his walk, too."

Robert's mouth dropped open. He couldn't believe what he was hearing.

"Don't forget these," his mother continued as she handed him the basket of muffins. "They're still warm — he'll like them."

Robert couldn't believe his mom was feeding Mr. Friggens *and* sending him to shovel his snow. It must be nice to be old.

Chapter 3

Sitting A Spell

As Robert passed Thor, the husky sniffed at the air and jumped at the end of his chain.

"You're always hungry, aren't you?" With his mittened hand, Robert reached under the napkin for one of the warm muffins and tossed it toward the dog. Thor leaped and snatched it from the air. With one gulp it was gone.

Mr. Friggens will never miss it, thought Robert. The words of his neighbor flashed through his mind. Mr. Friggens was right about Thor's career as a sled dog. When Robert's father was still able to compete in the sled races, Thor was always the strongest and smartest lead dog on any of the teams.

Robert began to feel even more sorry for himself. His father had promised to teach him how to drive a dogsled. That would never happen now — besides, Thor was too old to pull. Robert patted the dog. He knew he hadn't been ignoring Thor. Mr. Friggens should mind his own business.

After crossing the yards that separated the two houses, Robert found Mr. Friggens bundled up like a bear and leaning on his shovel. As Robert approached, the old man coughed and spit into a snow pile.

Gross! thought Robert. I'm glad I didn't walk that way.

"My mother asked me to bring these to you," Robert said to his elderly neighbor.

"What? I can't hear you. Speak up!"

Robert began again. "My mother asked me to bring these over to you. They're muffins." He held the basket out.

Mr. Friggens hesitated a moment, then took the basket with a quick jerk. With his other hand, he pushed the shovel toward Robert.

"Here," he said. "You're young; you can finish up."

Robert stood in surprise as the old man headed toward his house.

Mr. Friggens stamped the snow from his feet and entered the house, turning on an outdoor light.

Shaking his head at the old man's rudeness, Robert began to shovel. Adults always say kids don't have any manners. What about this guy? he thought.

Just then, Mr. Friggens poked his head out from behind the storm door. "Make sure you get it clean to the mailbox, and bring the shovel in when you're done," he instructed before yanking the door shut.

Robert walked out to the mailbox and started shoveling toward the house. Most of it was already done. It was clear to him that the old man was still strong. Where he'd shoveled, he had cleared the snow all the way to the concrete.

Determined to do as good a job as Mr. Friggens, Robert scraped at the walk and tossed the snow aside. As he worked, he caught glimpses of the old man through the window, busy at his fireplace.

When the walk was finished, Robert opened the storm door and knocked on the inside door. Not hearing an answer, he cautiously turned the knob and pushed it open, calling out to Mr. Friggens.

"Knock the snow off your feet and shut the door. What's the matter with you, son? Brought up in a mine?" The old man laughed. He was sitting in a worn chair close to the fireplace, smoking his pipe.

Not planning to stay, Robert left the door ajar behind him. "Where would you like your shovel, Mr. Friggens?"

"Shut the door. I'm not heating the outside here! Did you get it all done? All the way to the mailbox?"

Robert nodded and closed the door tightly.

"Don't want ice forming on the walk. When I go out to get the mail, I could break my neck."

"I got it down to the concrete. It should be fine."

"Put that shovel next to the door. I hope you knocked the snow off. Kids nowadays don't know how to do anything right."

"The snow's off the shovel. I made sure before I came in."

"Well, good!"

Robert thought it was surprising just how ornery Mr. Friggens could be. He carefully leaned the shovel next to the door. As he did, he noticed a pair of old ice skates hanging there. They had double runners and were made to strap onto boots.

"Take off your coat and boots and come sit a spell," said Mr. Friggens, motioning with his pipe. "Come on in here, son; I want to get a look at you.

"I remember the day your mother and father brought you home from the hospital. Your father was so proud, he brought you right over to show me."

"I can't stay long; I've got homework to do."

Mr. Friggens ignored Robert's protest. "Your father was a good man. Hard worker, he was, and a real champion with the sled and team."

It was nice to hear someone talking about his father that way. As he unlaced his boots, he noted that almost every bit of wall space in the tiny kitchen and adjoining living room was filled with things.

A stuffed owl and a stack of cigar boxes sat on one shelf. There was a large glass case filled with rocks, each with a small identification label. Pinned to the walls were pictures cut from magazines, most of them showing dog-sled teams or ice skaters. This house is like a museum, thought Robert, full of neat junk.

The old man noticed his interest. "The house isn't none too neat since my wife died, but all this stuff you see here has a story that goes with it," he said. "There isn't anything here I want to get rid of."

"I think it's cool," said Robert.

"Cool, I don't know, but it sure is cold outside! Come on in and sit down. Some hot soup will be good for your **innards**."

Mr. Friggens waved with his pipe toward the fireplace. On the raised hearth were two steaming bowls of soup, two mugs, and the basket of his mother's muffins.

"Well, I really shouldn't," said Robert. "My mother will be waiting for me to come home so we can have supper together."

"What's the matter, aren't you old enough to eat without your mother? Don't worry. I talked with her on the phone this afternoon. I told her I'd feed ya."

"You talked with my mom?" Feeling a bit betrayed, Robert plopped down on a dirty green pillow that had long ago lost its tassels.

In his overstuffed chair, Mr. Friggens took a last pull on his pipe. "You want a puff?" he asked, waving it in Robert's direction.

Robert smiled. In a way, he couldn't help liking the gruff old guy. He probably didn't mean to sound like a grouch; it was just a habit.

"No thanks. I don't smoke."

The old man nodded and knocked the ashes from the pipe into an ashtray. From his sweater pocket he pulled a set of false teeth. Holding them up to the light from the fire, he picked sweater fuzz off them, then wiped them with a napkin.

Robert watched in amazement as Mr. Friggens opened his mouth wide and popped in the upper set of teeth, pressing them tightly against his gums. Next the lower teeth went into place.

"There." The old man gave a big smile to show his teeth, then chattered them together to be sure they were secure. "Don't like wearing 'em all the time. Makes my mouth sore. I just use 'em when I eat, and keep 'em in my pocket the rest of the time."

What a funny old guy, thought Robert. Maybe someday I'll have teeth I can carry around in my pocket, too.

Mr. Friggens pulled back the napkin that covered the muffin basket and examined the contents. It was easy to see where a muffin had been removed. "Not an even number of muffins here. That's not like your mother," he commented. "It appears maybe somebody got a head start on me."

Robert tried not to look guilty.

The old man lifted out one of the little cakes and took a great, crumbling bite, chewing it with satisfaction.

"Your mother is some baker. Don't blame ya if you nipped one before you got here. I used to go down to the bakery before my shift every morning to get one of your mother's fresh blueberry muffins."

With crumbs falling every which way, some sticking to his unshaven face, Mr. Friggens smiled and picked bits of muffin from his sweater, putting them into his mouth.

"Don't just sit there," he said. "Help yourself. I've never seen a boy who wasn't hungry. Same as with dogs."

Robert wasn't sure he'd be able to eat if Mr. Friggens kept devouring things he found on his sweater. But the soup did smell good. He pulled a bowl to the edge of the hearth and slowly began to sip, blowing gently on each spoonful to cool it. It *was* good.

Chapter 4

Beginnings

"You know, son, there aren't too many things in this old world that a good cook like your mother can't fix. I wish she were around here, making bread and muffins for me."

Robert smiled. "Yeah, she is a good cook, but food doesn't always help. Especially if you go to school."

"School? I went to school 'til I was sixteen, got myself an eighth-grade education.

"School was different back then. We had a one-room schoolhouse with all the classes together in a big room. The young ones, they'd be reciting their ABC's. Others would be working on their penmanship or reading. We all had something different we were doing, all at the same time. And if you were a good student, it would be your job to help someone who was doing poorly."

Robert experienced a brief, unpleasant vision of Mary roaming around his classroom as Mrs. Runyon's little helper.

"How many students in your school?" asked Mr. Friggens.

Robert thought for a moment. "I don't know. Maybe two or three hundred."

"Two or three hundred? That's why they've got so much trouble in school today. My school, from the little bitty ones all the way to the top, didn't have more than twenty-five.

"You got a good-looking teacher?"

Robert paused again. He had never thought about how Mrs. Runyon looked. "Yeah, she's a good-looking lady," he finally decided with a grin.

"Well, my last teacher sure was good-looking. That was one of the reasons I showed up every day, just to get a look at that teacher! She had long black hair and big brown eyes . . . .

"And she wasn't much older than eighteen. I always thought maybe the two of us could get together sometime. I at least wanted to try and steal a kiss."

Robert laughed at the thought of kissing his teacher.

"Then I learned she was already spoken for and was going to get married," Mr. Friggens continued. "That was when I decided my time as a student was over. Anyway, I wasn't going to be anything special like a professor or anything.

"And the mines were waiting for me. I figured if I could read, write, and **cipher**, so I'd know if the company was cheating me on my pay, then I knew enough to get by."

Robert was shocked. He knew from his parents and from Mrs. Runyon that an education was one of the most important things in the whole world.

"My granddaddy was always after me to get more learning," the old man recalled. "He was a doctor, you know, and so was his father. Back then, many doctors got their learning by reading and hearing about cures from the old **herb women** and the Indians. They passed that knowledge down from one generation to the next."

After a long, dreamy look into the fire, Mr. Friggens turned to Robert.

"You holding a job yet? What are you, pretty close to sixteen?"

"No, I'm only twelve. I get an allowance and make some extra money raking leaves and stuff, but I don't have a regular job."

"Well, you're a tall one, I thought for sure you had to be close to sixteen. Twelve? Ha, you're still a pup, wet behind the ears.

"So, you're having problems in school? Don't you like it?"

Robert sat back from his soup. "I like it most of the time, but when I — well, it just seems as if I'm always in trouble. Like this extra assignment I got today. I've got to collect mining stories and make a report — five pages!"

"Well, that's not so hard. I got plenty of mining stories myself. I'm eighty-two now, so that's what — sixty-six years ago that I started working in the mines, just like my father.

"I spent the better part of forty-five years underground like a mole, digging out red iron ore. I'd come out covered from head to foot with red dust.

"When you work down in a hole, you don't even know what's going on outside. You don't know if it's day or night, if the sun is shining bright or if the old north wind blew up a blizzard. Lots of times I'd go to work when it was still dark, and when I came out it was dark again. I'd miss the whole day.

"The mine is cold, dark, and wet. I worked there, just like your father. It's a hard, dirty job.

CLINTON-MACOMB PUBLIC LIBRARY
SOUTH

"But today they got the big machinery above ground. I stopped by the **Cleveland** the other day, and they have trucks with wheels on them taller than this ceiling here. It was an amazing sight. Things have changed . . . . Things have changed a lot. And they say things are much better."

Mr. Friggens paused for another long look into the fire, and then went straight to the point. "Now — would you like me to help you out with your homework by telling you some mining stories?"

"That would be great," said Robert, enjoying his second mug of hot chocolate of the day. It suddenly occurred to him that his assignment might not be so unbearable after all.

"Here. You might be needing to take some notes." Mr. Friggens handed Robert a pencil and a small pad of paper that had been beside him in the chair.

"I keep these right here. When you get old, you've got to make lots of notes," he explained. "Then you usually forget where you put them." He chuckled.

"Maybe I should go home and get my question sheets that Mrs. Runyon gave me," said Robert.

Mr. Friggens turned gruff again. "I don't have all the time in the world to sit here doing nothing," he said. "If you want to hear some stories, fine. But I don't have time for fooling around with question sheets. Why don't you just listen and make notes?"

Robert quickly decided to agree.

"All right. Now where should I begin?"

"Why don't you start at the beginning of iron mining up here," Robert suggested.

"The beginning? That's a mighty tall order," chuckled the old man, picking up his own mug of chocolate.

"The beginning around here wasn't much to talk about. There was nothing but wilderness when iron mining first started.

"They say the rocky hills around here were covered with different kinds of trees, from evergreens to birch and maple. Some were so big that several men could link arms and not surround the trunks.

"Being that there was no lumbering here yet, the forests had never been cut. Of course, that would change — "

"We learned that Michigan and Wisconsin were both prime lumbering places at one time," Robert interrupted.

"Yep, you got that right. Lumbering and mining was what built this place. My family goes back to the 1850s around these parts. Back then, Marquette was a tiny settlement, just starting out. And there were Indians living all around. Most of the white people were Frenchies, French-Canadians who worked with what was left of the fur trade. Other folks thought the land up here was worthless since much of it couldn't be farmed. In fact, Michigan's leaders didn't really even want this **U.P.**

"Anyone ever tell you about the **Toledo War**, that made this land part of Michigan?"

"Wasn't that when the state traded a little strip of land along the Ohio border for the whole Upper Peninsula?"

"That's the one. Somebody's been teaching you right.

"Anyway, in the 1840s people began to change their minds about the U.P. A government **surveyor** named **William Burt** and his party were running a **boundary line** over by Negaunee."

Robert knew some of this story. "Wasn't that when their compasses went crazy and were swinging all over the place from the magnetic pull of the iron ore?"

"That's right. Burt told his men to look around, and they found rocks looking like bars of broken iron just lying on the ground. There was so much iron they had to use a **solar compass** to get their surveying done.

"When they went back down to Detroit, everyone got all excited. A group of businessmen put money together and sent another party up here to look for the iron, but they couldn't find it.

"It was an Indian named Marji Gesick who finally directed the men to an uprooted tree with red iron dust everywhere around it. But old Marji Gesick, he wouldn't come near the place — maybe because of his superstitions, or maybe so his people couldn't accuse him of showing strangers the iron.

"That land became the first mine. It was called the Jackson Mine, being as the biggest investors were from Jackson, Michigan.

"Anyway, from that time on, mining just grew and grew, stretching across the Upper Peninsula and into Wisconsin and Minnesota. We've got the Marquette Range here, and then the Menominee Range, and let's see — the Gogebic, and then the Mesabi and Vermilion ranges in Minnesota. This whole northern region is just loaded with ore."

"Do you know how to spell Mesabi?" Robert asked as he jotted notes.

"Just sound it out and look it up later," said Mr. Friggens.

"I don't even know if this is what I'm supposed to be doing for my assignment, but your stories are neat," Robert said. "How do you know all these things?"

The old man chuckled and picked up his pipe. From a can beside his chair he filled it, pushing the stringy tobacco down into its bowl. After striking a match, he puffed patiently, pulling the flame into the tobacco and producing gray curls of smoke. Then he settled back into his chair.

"I told you, I've got an eighth-grade education."

Chapter 5

Sault de Sainte Marie

"Well, I had a granddaddy who was one of the most interesting men you'd ever meet," said Mr. Friggens. "He was a real adventurer, he was. Wasn't afraid of nothing.

"He came up here when he was just a boy, about your age, in 1854. His name was Robert, too — some coincidence, wouldn't you say? He came by **canal boat** across New York State on the **Erie Canal**, all by his lonesome.

"His home had been in Albany, New York, but after his mother and little sister died of **cholera**, his father decided to move on. He'd probably heard of 'Iron Fever', which was much like 'Gold Fever'. About the same time men out west in California were panning for yellow metal, men here were digging for the red.

"Anyways, his father — my great-grandfather — left Albany and went to the Soo. The full name of the place was **Sault de Sainte Marie** then. You can look it up. He had heard there was a need for doctors in the U.P.

"He worked in the Soo for a while and then decided to settle farther west, in the new town of Marquette or 'Wooster,' as they used to call it. That one I know was spelled W-o-r-c-e-s-t-e-r, not much like the way it sounds, eh?

"So he sent for his son, my granddaddy. And that's how I came to be born up here in Michigan instead of New York State."

Pausing, Mr. Friggens put down his pipe and leaned forward for his soup. With great slurping sounds, he drank it directly from the bowl.

Robert was grateful for the pause. The fireplace at his side was warm and bright, and the generous portions of soup and muffins made him feel comfortable and content. Mr. Friggens had turned out to be a pretty good guy.

As he watched the fire, Robert was becoming deliciously sleepy. Waiting for Mr. Friggens to resume, he rested his arm on the hearth, then rested his head on his arm.

"Now, where'd I leave off? Oh — my granddaddy, left from Mackinac Island on a **schooner**. It was late fall, almost too late to be traveling, and he needed to reach the Soo quickly so he and his father could head for Marquette before the snow came . . . ."

Robert wondered if he could stay as comfortable as he was and still write notes. He felt the pencil slide from between his fingers as he began to drift off.

• • •

Fog had surrounded Mackinac Island for several days, keeping all ships at rest in its usually busy harbor. But this morning, before light, Robert had gotten word at his **boardinghouse** that the fog was lifting enough to sail the channel to Sault de Sainte Marie. He quickly packed his bag, more than ready for the last part of his long travels alone.

His father, Doctor James Friggens, had written him several letters over the last few months. He described the northern wilderness, the huge lock being built in Sault de Sainte Marie, as well as the puzzling illnesses he was attempting to treat. Robert longed to discover the wilderness for himself and to join his father for the adventures that lay ahead.

The schooner's sails snapped as they took the west breeze, and soon they were under way. Before they were far from the island, the fog lifted entirely as sunrise lit the horizon to the east.

After coasting by St. Martin Island, they entered the Cheneaux, or "Channels." Here the shipping lanes twisted and turned amid many small, low islands, most of them covered with cedar and birch. The trees were hung with moss, or lichen, giving the islands a mysterious appearance.

The ship sailed on, turning northward to pass between the mainland and Drummond Island, a much larger island than those Robert had seen so far.

The woman who ran the boardinghouse on Mackinac had told him that the British set up a post on Drummond after their last war with the Americans in 1812. But when the boundary between Canada and the United States was agreed upon, the island became part of the United States. The British had to move their post to St. Joseph Island, just to the north.

The schooner, under full sail, moved quickly northward. They passed island after island, which dotted the many bays and channels and gave this northern tip of Lake Huron a haunting beauty. Robert knew that the boundary line here curved between the islands, making some of them American, some Canadian.

As the day wore on, the waterway narrowed, becoming a river. Robert heard sailors say that Sault de Sainte Marie lay just ahead. The trip had gone quickly, but now the minutes seemed like hours. He and his father had been separated much too long.

From the foresail mast a warning bell clattered, directing passengers to gather their belongings. The first of the rapids — and the end of their voyage — were just ahead. Robert picked up his heavy **carpetbag**, which contained everything he owned, and began straining to see a familiar face among the people on the dock.

There was a hustle and bustle as people crowded one another for their place in line to leave the schooner. As Robert crossed the plank to the dock, goods from the ship were already being unloaded onto wagons by **Métis**. Not many years earlier, these short-legged, broad-shouldered men would have been using their muscles to power the large canoes used in the fur trade. But that industry had slowed considerably, and now their great strength earned them a living on the docks.

Robert scanned the crowd for a glimpse of his father, a tall, slight man with dark hair. Just then he heard a familiar voice.

"Robert. Robert!" There amid the noise and confusion stood his father, his arms spread wide in greeting.

Hauling his bag along as best he could, Robert ran to his parent. They met first with a great bear hug, then stood back to look at each other with smiles. The doctor recognized that his son had become a young man over these months they'd been apart. "It's about time you made it to the great North!" he said. "I've never been so glad to see anyone in my whole life.

"I got your aunt's post, saying she put you on the canal boat along the Erie. And I knew when cousin Dennis put you on the ship from Detroit to Mackinac. But after that I heard nothing, and I began to worry. I've been meeting every ship in search of you.

"Were you safe and well? Were people kind to you as you traveled? Was your **letter of credit and reference** accepted for your lodging?"

"Yes, Father. It went well, and I was fine." Robert was, however, grateful to be back with his father. His travels had made him appreciate a parent's care more than ever.

Wagons on the dock now began to move, forcing them to step aside.

"Come!" said his father as he picked up Robert's bag. "You have seen nothing like this before. Nothing can equal the sight of these men moving goods around the rapids, and the Indians and Frenchies shooting the rapids. There's even a **strap railway** here, the first one in the north country, with carts on rails being pulled by horses and mules."

"Like along the Erie Canal?"

"That's right. But first, let me show you the sault — that's another word for rapids."

Ahead, horses and mules slowly pulled wagons and carts along hilly roads. Men with whips drove the loads, making sure the animals kept a steady pull so they would not get stuck in the muddy track.

"These wagons are **portaging** goods around the rapids and falls," Doctor Friggens explained. "It isn't far, but the going can be rough, especially in rainy weather like we've had in the last few days."

Travelers who hadn't arranged passage aboard a wagon picked their way on foot up the muddy road beside the St. Mary's River. Ladies were particularly careful, lifting their long traveling skirts just high enough to keep them from the mud but still not show their ankles. Some of the children had hitched rides behind unguarded wagons, which pulled them sliding through the mud.

"Come look," called his father as they approached a clearing that overlooked the river. Below were rapids descending noisily toward the docks where Robert's ship had stopped. Bobbing in the wild, curling waters were some bark canoes.

"The St. Mary's River drains Lake Superior water into Lake Huron. The fall of the river is almost twenty-three feet, and most of that drop occurs in this half a mile.

"Of course, large boats cannot travel it; that's why the big lock is being built not far from here. Some Indians and Frenchies are skilled enough to go up the rapids with a half-loaded canoe, and they can return with full loads."

Robert watched the churning water pour through, boiling with foam as it was thrown violently in all directions by rocks and boulders. It was amazing to see the canoes darting through it to carry goods upriver.

"I wouldn't want to be in one of those canoes right now," his father commented after a few minutes. "Come, we must hurry. A storm is on its way."

Robert could feel the wind rising. Small trees along the pathway began to wave and dance, and dark clouds soon blocked the setting sun. As the sky grew more threatening, they heard a heavy roll of thunder from the west.

He and his father walked quickly down the road until they caught up with a mule cart. For a few pennies, the driver allowed the two of them to hop onto the back.

From the cart, Robert watched half-naked men, wet from the wind-whipped river, pulling bark canoes onto the shore. When they overturned the canoes on land, dozens of large fish spilled out.

"Those Indians make their living by fishing for the fur companies, the mining companies, and the workers building the lock," said Robert's father. "They also dry and smoke fish so they can survive during the winter. Their people have fished here for more than a thousand years.

"Those fish are called 'Mackinaw trout' or whitefish. People here serve it boiled in a broth and add maple syrup. It is one of my favorite meals, and I'm sure you'll like it, too."

From the road, Robert could see and smell fish that were stretched out to dry on wooden frames. He wasn't happy about the prospects of countless meals of fish.

Flashes of lightning lit the sky as the cart rounded a curve and entered the settlement of Sault de Sainte Marie. Just as the cart stopped in front of a small, two-story frame house, they felt the first big drops of a cold rain.

"Here we are," his father said, jumping down. "This is my boardinghouse. Hurry!" He and Robert ran through the gate of a picket fence to the porch of the gray, weathered house. As they opened the door, Robert smelled hot food and felt the warmth of a wood fire. A white-haired, gentlemanly old fellow with a curly mustache greeted them from the parlor.

"Come in, come in. This must be your son we have heard so much about." The man extended his hand to Robert.

"Robert, this is Mr. Whitaker," said James. "He owns this house and has been a fine friend."

Mr. Whitaker smiled with the compliment. "You are just in time for some hot stew and yellow bread. You must be hungry after your trip. Is there any news from Mackinac worth hearing?

Robert, who had not paid much attention to the adult talk around Mackinac, shrugged his shoulders. "I don't believe so, sir." He looked expectantly into the dining room where a large table was already set.

"Well, no news is to be considered good news, I have always been told," said Mr. Whitaker, excusing himself to go to the kitchen.

"Here, Robert," said his father. "You can hang your things near the fire to dry. Mrs. Whitaker is visiting her sister and will not be home this evening. Things are a little more casual when she is away."

Robert smiled, remembering some of his mother's rules. She had run a very fit house — and it was always certain that your coat was to be hung on the coat tree by the door.

As Robert warmed himself, one memory led into another. He still missed his mother and younger sister, both taken in a few days by a disease his father could do nothing about.

Now his father was determined to help put an end to cholera. That desire had led the doctor to the Sault, where an outbreak of the disease six months earlier had killed **scores** of the men working on the lock. No one quite understood the illness which now seemed to have left the area as unexpectedly as it had arrived.

Mr. Whitaker returned to the dining room with corn bread and two steaming bowls on a tray. "It's **venison** stew," he said. "Come find a place. The others will soon be here."

Robert quickly remembered how hungry he was and pulled out a chair at one end of the table.

"We should wash first, Robert. Washing is the way to stay healthy," his father instructed. He picked up Robert's carpetbag and led the way up the narrow staircase near the front door.

"This is one of the largest boardinghouses along the Superior shore," his father said. "Very small compared with those in Albany, wouldn't you say?"

Entering one of the rooms, James put down the bag and felt around in the dark. "There should be **strikers** here on the mantel for the lamp. I usually come up to the room before dusk and set a fire, so it's warm and I have light later on."

Soon he found the matches and struck one on the mantel's edge. Removing the clear glass chimney of an oil lamp, he lit the cloth wick, then turned a knob to shorten it. The wick burned brightly enough to light the room with a red-orange glow.

The room was not large, but it would do for the two of them. Opposite a small fireplace stood a high bed. Near the bed was a washstand with a plain cream-colored pitcher and bowl.

"You get washed, while I set the fire," his father said.

Robert poured cold water from the pitcher into the bowl and rubbed his hands together in it. Shadows prevented him from seeing how much dirt he had washed off.

"Get your face and neck as well. This might be the north country, but the Whitakers like everyone to be presentable at their table. And remember, gentlemen show their breeding by how clean they keep themselves."

Robert rubbed water on his face, neck, and behind his ears, then used a small linen towel hanging beside the washstand to dry himself. By that time the fire was well started and James took his turn at the washstand.

As they descended the stairs, Robert heard voices from the dining room. At the table they found two men eating the meals Mr. Whittaker had offered them earlier.

"I told them to get to eating, since you two would be a few minutes," Mr. Whitaker explained. He went to the kitchen and soon returned with bread and two more portions of stew.

After being introduced to the men, Robert learned they were here to work on the new lock, which was to open the next year.

"The grandest undertaking ever attempted by man, or beast," said one.

"Not as grand as the Erie Canal," Robert responded jokingly.

"The Erie Canal? Why, this lock will be in use long after the gates to the Erie are closed," said Mr. Whitaker. "This is the most important undertaking ever on this continent. It will open navigation and the doors of the iron industry to the world."

"If old Shegud gets out of the way and lets it happen," commented one of the workers.

"He cannot stop progress," said the other.

"Shegud is a chief of the Saulteurs, or Chippewa Indians," Robert's father explained to him. "It seems that the engineers and surveyors chose what they thought was the best place for the lock. They mapped it out and the plan was accepted by the government. When construction began, however, they discovered the lock was being dug right through the middle of an ancient Indian cemetery."

Robert paused with a spoonful of stew midway between his bowl and his mouth. From everything he knew of his father, Robert was certain that he believed in the rights of all people and would favor the Indians in this case.

"Shegud won't change the way things need to be by standing out in the cold, disputing the workers, and chanting his old prayers," said one of the workers.

"I agree," said Mr. Whitaker. "The Indians may have been here first, but they did nothing to improve the land. Then the Frenchies came with their boats full of furs, and still there was no improvement.

"When we Americans came, we put our backs to the plow, cut the land, planted seeds, and made a settlement grow. The people who came before have to make way for progress. Iron ore from the western ranges has to be carried out by ship — even if it means the Indians lose their sacred burial grounds."

After that speech, Robert's food didn't taste very good. This was the "fine friend" his father had introduced? These men seemed to have poor opinions of anyone different from themselves. He put down his spoon and followed his father upstairs.

"Father, why do those men dislike the Indians so?" he asked when they were in their room.

"It's their way. And it's not just the Indians. They would dislike anyone who got in the way of bringing progress and riches to this land.

"It is said that 'money is the root of all evil,' and I think we have heard an example of that this evening. Money causes greedy men to do terrible things and make bad decisions."

Robert removed his traveling clothes and hung them over the chair. Still in his long underwear, he crawled under the big quilt and settled into the **feather tick** on the bed.

Robert only hoped that as his adventure continued, he would not meet many people like those he had met this evening. Even with the steady rain, he could still hear gruff, harsh voices from below as he faded off to sleep.

Chapter 6

The Welcome

The next morning, Robert yawned and stretched in the big feather bed. The rain had stopped, and through the window he could see a beautiful sunrise.

His father, already washed and dressed, was about to carry their bags downstairs. "It's about time you made your appearance," he teased as Robert sat up in bed. "When you are ready, go down and get yourself some tea and a bowl of hot oats off the back of the stove. It could be a long time before we will have the chance to take hot food again."

Robert quickly got ready. Downstairs, the house was quiet. From the dining room he could see Mr. Whitaker out in the yard, chopping wood for his fireplaces.

Robert entered the kitchen and took a bowl from a stack on the table. On the back of the big cookstove stood a large pot with a wooden spoon sticking out. The oats were so stiffly cooked that he had to use a finger to scrape them off the big spoon and into his bowl. As thick as these oats were, he thought, they should stick to him for the rest of the month.

After he added some cream from a pitcher and a sprinkle of **maple sugar** from a jar beside the stove, the oats made a tolerable breakfast. He was just finishing as his father brought down the last of his medical bags.

"I guess we're ready," James said. "I'll settle up my bill and hire a cart for these things.

"I thought you might want to walk and get a look at this place. If you follow the roadway, you'll come to where the lock is being built. The next time you get a chance to see it, it will be probably be filled with water. I will get our things to the dock and meet you at the construction. Is that agreeable?"

Robert nodded. After returning his empty bowl to the kitchen Robert left the boardinghouse on foot.

The road to the main part of town continued along the waterway, and he could see several fishing canoes already at work in the morning sun. This promised to be a good day for travel, especially now that he would be with his father.

He passed two smaller boardinghouses and then a hotel, where men in suits sat by the front windows eating breakfast. This must be for businessmen passing through, he thought; he had seen similar places along the Erie Canal and in Detroit.

Farther along the road, along with frame houses and cabins, were an **icehouse**, a milk house, several large storage barns, stables, and a woodworking shop. Some of the buildings showed signs of having been whitewashed at one time, but most had been weathered by the winds to about the same shade of gray. A windmill in great need of some grease shrieked as it turned in the breeze.

Robert tried to imagine what this place would have looked like earlier. It had probably been covered by trees, he thought, with Indian camps strung along the water. The river would have been "main street" back then.

As the breeze picked up, Robert felt the chill of late fall through his wool suit. He was glad he had worn his cap and not packed it in his bag. It was always better to bet toward wellness than to challenge sickness, his father liked to say.

Walking on, Robert heard the lock construction before he could see it. There were sounds of men, lots of men. He heard sledge hammers striking iron, axes biting into wood, and picks shattering rock.

Then he could see it. It was an immense opening in the ground, a ditch so large and deep that from where Robert stood, he could not see the men working at its bottom. He knew now why everyone called it the great lock.

With its high wooden sides, Robert decided the lock looked like an enormous cradle set in the earth. Men used pulleys to lower supplies in nets to the bottom. On each end of the lock were pairs of huge wooden doors that would pen the water in or keep it out as ships were raised or lowered.

The noise of the workers below echoed from the walls, making ghostly sounds that suddenly reminded Robert of the Indians who had been buried here. He looked around in the commotion, thinking he might see Chief Shegud. Instead everyone he saw seemed intent on finishing the work so the lock could open in the spring.

Robert recalled the little cemetery plot in New York where his mother and sister were buried. A shudder passed through him at the thought of anyone digging up their graves.

At that moment a large red-tailed hawk glided over Robert, then beat the air with its strong wings to climb higher into the sky. "Where'd you come from?" Robert said aloud in surprise, watching the graceful bird until it disappeared into the sun.

Robert blinked and rubbed his eyes. Everywhere he looked he saw big red spots. "The sun sure is bright," he said to himself. As he regained his sight, he noticed a beautiful red-brown feather lying near him. It must have come from the hawk.

Robert carefully picked it up and ran its delicate edge through his fingers. Removing his cap, he pressed the feather's quill into a seam so he could wear it above his ear.

"The lock is an amazing sight, isn't it?" said his father, who had come up behind him. "Where did you get the feather?"

Robert started to explain, but his father interrupted. "We'll have to hurry. The ship will be leaving soon. But that feather is a good sign. You are being welcomed by this land."

Father and son set off on the road to the dock.

Chapter 7

Mr. Shane

The schooner that awaited the Friggens was larger than the last one Robert had been on. As they crossed the gangplank, it appeared to Robert that many of the passengers were heading west to make new homes. Just as he had on the first part of his journey, Robert heard many accents and saw people of different races.

There were Irish, with their quick tongues, and English, who often left the ends off their words. He heard the deliberate speech of Africans, who might be escaping slavery in the South. The language of the French made everything sound like a question, and some people with German or Scandinavian backgrounds replaced their "W's" with "V's."

There were also Italians, talking rapidly and waving their hands in all directions. They always sounded to Robert as if they were arguing. Yet earlier, along the Erie Canal, he had watched a couple who appeared to be angry, and in another instant they were smiling at each other.

He thought about one of his father's favorite expressions, "You can't judge a book by its cover." He smiled thoughtfully. In his recent travels he had already seen an entire library of books, each with a different cover.

"It's nice to see so many families traveling this way — Finnish, Norwegians, Africans, Germans, Italians, Cornish, and the French-Indian Métis." Robert's father seemed to read his mind. "That means the country will grow."

"This place we are going to, is it called Marquette or is it Worcester?" Robert asked. "I hear you say one name, then you say the other."

"Well, the settlement first started as an Indian town, but when the Easterners began to arrive, they called it New Worcester. I am uncertain about the reason for that name, but — "

"I know the answer ta that, lad," said a rough-looking man in a dirty suit with a black kerchief tied around his broad neck. He walked stiffly to join them at the rail of the ship. With a big hand he rubbed his unshaven face, as if sizing up Robert and his father.

"Allow me ta introduce meself," he said, forcefully putting out a hand. "My name is Michael Shane, a

Cornish Cousin Jack as they say; I say a Cussin'
Jack. From Cornwall, England, I am. Even though I
call this here American shore me home now, I still
honor me motherland.

"The name 'New Worcester,' by gads, came from
Worcester, Massachusetts, the home of Amos R.
Harlow. He was the first to **cross lots** ta this
forsaken country we are travelin' to. The settling of
this place has not been so long ago that some of us
can't blasted well remember and acknowledge the
corn — if ya be knowin' me meaning in that."

Robert looked at his father in utter puzzlement.

"Ya see, Harlow established a post office in 1849
and named the place like his home in the East. The
trouble with that, those first settlers didn't know the
county and township had already been surveyed and
named for the almighty explorer and Jesuit father,
Jacques Marquette. If any of them would have
cared ta learn, they would have found the land was
called by his name as early as '43. And still t'day
there are some who call it by the one name and
some by the other. But Marquette is the proper
name.

"Ta this day ol' Amos Harlow is considered the
founder, the biggest frog in the puddle, even though

he didn't know beans where he was. Harlow produced the first iron **bloom** there, and just this last year he joined his Marquette Iron Company with the Cleveland Iron Company, all on one stick. Their money and work keeps this land and its people busy."

The schooner had finished loading and now left the dock. Soon sails on both its masts were filling with wind, and the water glistened with the sun's reflection.

"By the old man's beard, she sure is pretty, this lake," said Michael Shane. "And just like a beautiful woman, she's dangerous, this one is. In just another few weeks, when the gales come blowin', she will hear no excuse for anyone caught on her waters.

"The **Three Sisters of the Lake**, they could lick right over the sides of any ship, be it big or small, and take every man, woman, and child with them back into the great freshwater sea. There's been many a ship curse 'em, they've taken under."

Robert was hearing more oaths and curse words than he had heard in his whole life. It fascinated him the way Mr. Shane could string strong words together, like an artist painting a picture.

Robert noticed, however, that when other travelers got within earshot of "Cornish Cussin' Jack" ladies' mouths would drop open and parents moved their young children away. Even James watched his son closely to make sure he wasn't enjoying the speaking habits of their new acquaintance too much.

The schooner first took a north-by-northwest heading. Mr. Shane pointed out Gros Cap, on the Canadian side, and Point Iroquois, on the American, standing like pillars of granite to guard the mouth of mighty Superior.

"Don't they remind ya, by Moses, of two tall ladies standin' to bid ya farewell?" he sighed.

As Robert looked away with a grin, his father put a hand on his shoulder to remind him to be mannerly.

Once past the pillars, the lake spread like a great sea before them, and spray from the cold waves of Superior occasionally kicked over the rail, bringing squeals from women and children.

"Ya see those bitty boats there, bobbin' in the lake?" The Cornish man pointed to tiny dots hugging close to the American shoreline. "Well, in another month it would mean their deaths to be out here.

Even the big ore boats, dash them, won't take the chance if they are smart.

"I would be believin' that those canoes are full of fur from Wisconsin, making for the Sault de Sainte Marie before the weather turns.

"When I first came ta this forsaken land, there were lots of traders still workin' and trappin'. Now, with the lumberin' and the mines, there's other work ta be had."

"Are there lots of mines where we are going?" Robert asked.

"More than ya can shake a stick at. They open for a few years and then close just as quick — especially if there's been a bad accident. Sometimes they close because the ore gives out, or the owners' money gives out.

"I've lived around mines all my life. First in Cornwall, where the earth crumbled beneath our houses because of the caves below, and now here in the cold north country."

"I would like to be a miner and find gold or silver or iron," Robert said.

"Blast, boy, who has been talkin' with ya?" Mr. Shane almost exploded. "There ain't no fun down in those holes, riskin' yer life for six or seven cents an hour.

"I worked in the mines at yer age. I was a **ruffian** with the rest, pullin' out wheelbarrows full of stone. In a mine, yer in the bowels of the earth. The water gathers, and it's black and cold.

"Ya stick a candle in yer **cap lamp** and pray that six candles will get ya through a shift. If not, ya have ta find yer way out of the hole in blackness.

"If ya work in a dry hole, yer lucky. Most have to stand knee-deep in cold water all day, pullin' out the ore. I was a mucker for a time, diggin' out the ore and dirt with a shovel. Hard, back-breakin' work that was. Ya always had a sore back, but never let on, so ya wouldn't be replaced.

"Then I worked as a teamster for a while, drivin' the mules that move ore cars around down in the hole. That was a good bit easier on the back."

"It must have been hard getting those mules down there every day," said Robert.

"What ya mean, every day? Once ya got the mule teams underground, ya left 'em down there. They ate and slept below, and it was not often that any came back out before they were retired or died.

"No, the mines are no place for the likes of you. After a while they were no place for the likes of me either. I pulled so many men from the mines as cold as a wheel rim that they called me the director."

"Director?" asked Robert.

"Director — the undertaker, boy. You don't want to work in the hole. Too many men die in those pits, makin' other men rich. That was why I got out and found work at the **charcoal camp**. You should come pay me a visit; a smart boy like yourself should have his future above ground."

Robert hadn't thought about the darkness and the dampness and the danger that went with being a miner. It no longer sounded good to him.

Getting tired of standing, Robert went and sat with his father, who had found shelter from the wind on a small bench. Michael Shane followed and proceeded to sit down next to them on the deck.

Robert stood immediately, saying, "Here, Mister Shane, you can have my place." His father nodded with pride at his son's good manners.

"Mister Shane, Mister Shane — blast, who is this Mister Shane?" said their new friend. "That was me father's name, dash ya, and he's gone to meet his maker these twenty years already. Call me Michael or Cussin' Jack, and stop this 'mister' business.

"You sit yerself on that bench — do I look like a **dandy**? I'm as strong as ten good men, and maybe a mule thrown in besides.

"You'd better sit. A soft boy like yerself from the East will need all the coddling this wilderness can afford."

Taken aback by this insult, Robert looked to his father, who by now had leaned back and had his eyes closed. But Robert was sure he saw a smile on his lips.

Mr. Shane barely paused for breath. "Boy, where'd ya get that fancy feather in yer cap? Was it a gift from some pretty little Indian girl at the Sault? Or did the Creator himself swoosh down from the heavens and drop it at your feet?"

Robert paused, remembering the hawk, but again missed his chance to tell about it.

"No explanation needed, boy. By Jove, no matter how ya got it, it's good medicine, as the Indians would say."

"My father's a doctor; did you know that?"

"A doctor, eh? So Worcester — excuse me, Marquette — will have itself a doctor full time. That's good medicine, too. We once had a doctor who got his learnin' from a school in Vermont. Don't know what happened to him. Maybe the weather was such that the East invited him back," Michael said as he chuckled to himself.

"I sure hope ya can take the **wrathy** cold of the North, 'cause it will test all ya have and then some."

"Winter is my favorite season," Robert replied. "I never get cold, and I like being outside."

"Well, boy, if ya can whip the cold here, this is going ta be the perfect place for ya ta live."

As the ship rounded Whitefish Point, the crew scurried to raise and lower sails, preparing to **tack** westward against the wind.

"If they're not cautious of the wind, it can chaw the sails up **catawampitously**," Michael said. "Anything that challenges the strength of Mother Nature up here, or Mother Earth as the natives say it, is bound to be the loser."

As Robert watched the passing shoreline, he closed his jacket across his chest and pulled his cap lower over his ears against the sharp air. Michael fell silent, pulling his work hat down over his eyes and stretching his legs in front of him on the deck.

Mr. Shane was sure an interesting character, Robert thought. He wondered if there would be more like him where they were going.

Comfortable in the roll of the ship, Robert joined his father and Mr. Shane in dozing off.

Waking later, he found himself lying lengthwise on the bench with Mr. Shane's thick jacket over him. His father and Mr. Shane stood talking together at the ship's rail.

Robert joined the men and thanked Mr. Shane for his jacket.

"Well, boy, ya slept too long, snorin' like a deck hand, too, and ya missed the almighty sand mountain," said Mr. Shane.

"It was quite a sight, son," said his father. "A mountain of sand, taller than any we have ever seen. Are you hungry? You slept for quite a while."

"An' tell him how he snored so loud, the ladies were all afraid ta come to this end of the deck because they thought a wild bear had swum out and climbed aboard."

Robert's face reddened in embarrassment.

"It wasn't quite that bad," his father laughed. "Mister Shane and I — "

"Please, I told ya, James, please call me Michael."

"Michael and I have been sharing a lunch Mr. Whitaker put together. There is more than enough left, so help yourself."

His father handed him a cloth bundle in which Mr. Whitaker had tied their food, and Robert returned to the bench. In the bundle were apples, thick slices of bread, and hard yellow cheese, along with boiled eggs in their shells and day-old **dunkers**, just hard enough to travel well.

Robert ate until he could eat no more, but he was thirsty. He saw Mr. Shane drinking from a small bottle he carried with him, something he'd also seen other men doing in his travels. After tying up the remaining food in the cloth, he returned the bundle to his father.

"Mr. Shane — "

Michael turned to Robert. "Wasn't aware me father had joined us," he said.

"Excuse me," said Robert, starting over. "Michael, could I please have a drink from your bottle?"

A big grin broke across Michael's face, and he gave a hearty laugh. "Sure, you can have a taste of me **anti-fogmatic** ta wet yer whistle, but I don't think your father would like it none."

James smiled at Robert. "Michael's drink is not something for you. You'll find a water pail and dipper up forward."

Embarrassed again, Robert realized that Mr. Shane had been drinking **hard spirits**. He made his way to the front of the ship, stepping carefully as it rose and fell with the waves. In the bow he found a wooden bucket with a dipper attached to it.

Robert helped himself to a clean, cold drink and was just returning the dipper to the bucket when the ship headed steeply into a wave and a shower of water crashed over him. He was so surprised by the unexpected soaking, that he failed to move for a second wave that splashed over the deck. Drenched and laughing, he ran back to his father and Mr. Shane.

"Thirsty indeed, were you? Not ta worry, you'll dry soon in this wind," said Mr. Shane.

Before long Robert's father pointed toward shore. "Look, son."

Running along the coastline as far ahead as they could see were brilliantly colored rock cliffs, at least a hundred feet high.

"Those are the Pictured Rocks, or some say Painted Rocks," Mr. Shane said. "Those walls might be a thing of beauty, but don't let a canoe be caught near 'em with a storm coming on. There is no place ta seek shelter or get off the water — you'll be dashed ta pieces."

The series of bluffs continued for miles. There were overhanging rocks and towers, waterfalls and water-worn caves. What Robert found most fascinating was the variety of colors in the rock. There were all hues of black and brown, sharply contrasting with yellow, red, pure white, and gray.

"See why I call it a cathedral?" said Mr. Shane. "It always reminds me of something I once heard:

Their rocky summits, split and rent,

Form'd turret, dome, or battlement,

Or seemed fantastically set

With cupola or minaret—

"That's Scott, from *The Lady of the Lake*."

"What does all that mean?" Robert asked as he and his father shared a surprised glance. It appeared that Michael Shane, at one time, had come by some education. But his manners certainly didn't give that away.

"It means, me boy, that thar ain't nothing in the old world that is more beautiful than this old pile o' rocks before ya. It's truly an almighty sight, more beautiful than anything made by the hands of men."

"It seems as if the water, many, many years ago, was much higher, judging by the lines on the cliffs — wouldn't you say so, Michael?" asked James.

"If I were a bettin' man, I'd say yer right about that, James. Forty, fifty feet higher, maybe more."

"Look," James said to Robert. "There, coming out from the wall of the cliff. There are four, no, five stone pillars supporting an arch. And there on the sides, more arches stretching out from it.

"They look like the pillars at the State House in Albany. Aren't they magnificent?"

Robert looked in awe at the walls of stone. Even with their great size and strength, he noticed, they curved and sloped gracefully, molded in a variety of designs and forms.

"Are there rocks like this where we're going?" he asked.

"Well, there are rocks, but not like these," Michael returned. "You'll see soon enough."

The sky's color began to soften, and before long the round flame of the sun dipped into the lake ahead of them, leaving a brief blaze of bright orange and shades of pink. Before the display was entirely gone, a bright red glow covered the ceiling of the earth.

"Red sky at night, sailors delight. Red sky at morning, sailors take warning," said Michael. "Should be a good day tamorrow."

Soon darkness covered the water. Robert, his father, and Michael made their way to the forward part of the schooner. Below deck were wooden shelves, called berths, with straw ticks that served as beds.

Robert and his father found an empty berth and crawled in, sharing their body heat under a thin blanket. As Robert tried to get comfortable, he heard Mr. Shane muttering about "squalling brats" and the stink of the ship.

Mr. Shane was right about both, thought Robert as he tried to block out the cries of children and the smell of overfilled **thunderpots**.

Robert and his father slept fitfully. By morning, they would be at their home port.

Chapter 8

Iron Bay

At daylight, Robert and his father were awakened by the clatter of the bell on the masthead. "We must have reached Marquette," said James. "What I wouldn't give for a basin of warm water to wash up, so as to greet our new home properly."

Robert ran his tongue around his teeth, trying to polish them. His father was right he thought: it is important to make a good first impression.

"Try to pull yourself together as best you can. I will locate our bags and meet you on deck. Here, this will help your teeth and breath. It's what's left of our lunch." He handed Robert an apple.

Robert pocketed the apple and began trying to make himself presentable. Pulling up the blanket, he found his cap and carefully straightened his feather before putting the cap on his head.

As he left the sleeping compartment, Robert realized that nearly all the other passengers were already on deck. Hurrying above, he found people gathering in lines with their baggage and children.

"Thar ya are, boy," Michael Shane called to him. "Didn't want ta leave without tellin' ya it was a pleasure ta make yer acquaintance. We will be allowed onto the dock soon."

"I was afraid we'd have to leave you behind," James joked to his son as he joined them.

The ship's bell clattered once more as the rope to the plank was released and passengers began to crowd off.

"Our bags, along with the medical supplies, are up front," James told his son. "I didn't want to take a chance that anything would get damaged with all these people milling about."

"When the way is clear, I'll give ya a hand with yer things," said Michael.

As they began to leave the ship, Michael insisted on helping them move the bags and equipment the length of the **corduroy** dock and onto the beach.

"Well, Michael, it has certainly been our pleasure to have met someone like yourself," James said as the last crate was deposited on the beach. "Your guided tour made the trip very pleasurable."

"I liked your stories," Robert added.

"Blast, man, it weren't nothing. It was doubly a pleasure ta have met the two of you. I'm supervisor up at the charcoal camp, an' I got a feeling I'll be payin' ya frequent visits."

"Well, you will be welcomed. I don't yet know where we will be staying. The community is providing a home for us."

"Oh, you two won't be hard ta find. You'll be the buzz of the town for many weeks to come," said Michael, offering his big hand to shake. "I've got to get going. Need ta check the post before I make me tramp ta the camp."

The ship's arrival had created a flurry of activity in the small harbor. Some passengers loaded their goods on wagons, while others greeted family and friends with hugs and happy chatter. Still others, perhaps alone in a new land, walked with their baggage toward the settlement.

Robert looked around. In the nearby town, the wind flattened plumes of gray smoke that came from a collection of small, wood-framed buildings. Some of the buildings had been whitewashed. Most of them, however, were weathered gray, looking far older than their years.

The commotion created by the arrival of a flat-bed wagon turned Robert's attention back to the harbor area.

"Excuse me," called a man, who wore spectacles and a tall, black silk hat and was accompanied by a small group of women. "Would you happen to be the eminent Doctor James Friggens and son?" His manner of speech and his appearance gave the man an air of authority.

"Sir, I am Doctor Friggens, and this is my son, Robert," James answered.

"I am pleased to make your acquaintance," said the man, climbing down from the wagon. "I am Reverend William Northland, and this is my daughter, Mary Margaret."

A tall, slim young woman with curly brown hair and warm dark eyes stepped forward. With a small curtsy she smiled at James, but their eyes met only briefly before she reddened and looked away. "Pleased to make your acquaintance," she said softly.

"And these are ladies of my church who have come to welcome you to our settlement," Rev. Northland continued. Robert noted that each of the matronly group before him held a basket of canned food and baked goods.

Just then Michael Shane pushed his way into the welcoming circle. Before Robert could greet him,

Rev. Northland said sternly: "Ruffian! Where are your manners?"

"Pardon me, Rev'rend, I was just admirin' this wonderful land of **calico** I find before me," said Michael. "It's enough ta set my cap ta spark."

"You, sir, are out of your place," said the reverend in a disgusted manner. Michael winked at Robert before moving on, but before Robert could return a knowing grin, he felt his father's elbow in his side.

"That man is an abomination to this community." Rev. Northland straightened his hat and pushed his glasses back up to the bridge of his nose before continuing.

"The ladies want to make you right at home. We are all happy to have a trained doctor in our midst, and are pleased that you arrived before the weather turns any worse. After another week or two, you would have been delayed until spring."

The ladies nodded and smiled in agreement, their cheeks rosy from the wind.

"We are also glad to get here now," James said. "My son joined me at the Sault only two days ago, so we could travel here together."

"As you have no doubt heard, we have had many bouts of fevers, typhoid, cholera, and all manner of other maladies over the last few years — not to mention mining accidents," said the reverend. "But let us not stand around any longer in this sharp wind. We should be getting you to your residence."

The ladies placed their gifts of food on the wagon and said their goodbyes. "The women will be taking turns, when their households permit, to do your housekeeping and cooking," said Rev. Northland as he helped James and Robert load their baggage.

"This horse and wagon, or my carriage, will be available to you when you have need. They are kept not far from you, and are yours for the asking."

James pulled himself up onto the wagon seat and helped Robert up. Mary Margaret hopped onto the wagon bed with the help of her father.

"Here, miss, excuse my rudeness. Please take this seat," said James.

"No, thank you, sir — "

"Please call me James."

"No, thank you, James, then," she said with another flash of crimson across her cheeks. "I will be fine here."

Rev. Northland boarded the wagon, and as he slapped the reins the horse pulled toward town. The road was narrow and muddy, but here and there stretches of wooden planking showed the settlement's intention to improve its hold on this land.

The wagon stopped near the crest of a small hill. In a hollow stood a modest frame house with two full stories under a peaked roof.

"This house is for your use, free and clear of expense. The bulk of your staples will be provided, and firewood as well, by the local families. The settlement will also give you a cash **stipend** every quarter to help with improvements." Rev. Northland recited the information in a formal manner. Then with more warmth he added, "On behalf of our people — welcome."

"I notice we have an herb garden," James said as he approached.

"Yes, Doctor," said Mary Margaret. "I harvest most everything myself. They are bundled and drying on the beams of your office. I do hope you use some of the old cures — that they are not too old-fashioned for you?"

James smiled at her sincerity. "Most of my healing is done with tried-and-true cures," he said.

"Of course, I read of new remedies in every journal I see. But I am most comfortable using the old ways of both the herb women and the Indians."

Pleased, Mary Margaret began to relate the local medicines that would be available to him.

"There are walnut leaves for **anemia**, wild clover tops for the blood and for **asthma**, catnip for **colic**, balsam fir sap for burns — "

"Sap for burns?" James interrupted.

"Oh yes, it works wonderfully. The Indians taught me that."

"It makes me wonder why this community would have need for me when it already has such an amazing young woman as yourself available."

As she blushed, her father said, "Mary Margaret is educated. She teaches school just down the road. Perhaps when you are settled, the boy might visit."

Robert wasn't so sure about school, but he liked the idea of meeting people his own age.

Rev. Northland led the climb up an outside stairway to the second floor where Robert and his father would live. They entered a sitting room with a fireplace and a fire already laid. **Rag carpets** covered the floor, and a small sofa and two chairs gave the room a comfortable feel. Off the sitting room were the kitchen and a small bedroom.

"Up the stairs from the sitting room, there is an attic room where the boy can sleep," said Rev. Northland. "If the door to the stairs is left open, I am told, the heat from below will warm the room nicely."

"Do you want to go look?" asked James.

Robert nodded and dashed up the stairs. The room was dark with only one small window. When Robert's eyes adjusted to the darkness, he found that the room he would call his own was large and mostly unfinished. Rag carpets covered most of the rough floor. There was a dresser and a small bed draped with a thick quilt and heavy black bearskin.

From below, Robert could hear the reverend continuing the tour. Racing back down the stairs to the sitting room, he nearly knocked Mary Margaret from her feet as she bent to light the fire.

"You shouldn't run in a home; it is very rude," she said sharply. Robert didn't know if he had simply startled her or if this was the real Mary Margaret.

"Excuse me," he said politely before following the men into the large kitchen. It held a great iron bake stove, a table with six chairs, and many cupboards. Off the kitchen was a staircase to the level below.

They descended the stairs to a large room that would be his father's office. It contained a chair and table for use as a desk, along with wall cabinets and a bookcase — things a doctor would need for his study and practice. On one wall was a fireplace, also with a fire already laid. And among the beams above their heads were **whisks**, twists, and bundles of dried herbs, as Mary Margaret had said.

"Your daughter is an asset to your community," James remarked.

"She is an asset to *our* community, Doctor. I hope you will soon think of this place as your home," said the reverend.

Robert noticed two other small rooms off the main room and went to investigate as Rev. Northland and his father chatted. They were evidently to be used as sickrooms. Each contained a cot dressed with white sheets and a small table and chair. Robert was sure this place had been built for a previous doctor.

A door in the main room led outdoors, just beside the herb garden. Robert went out and began carrying some of his father's bags into the office.

There was his medical kit, with its small glass **vials** of medicine, and his box of glass suction devices for **cupping**. James had also brought many of his own herbs, carefully dried and packaged. In addition there was a collection of instruments that were nearly all familiar to Robert, for he had always been interested in his father's work.

Robert knew his father dreamed of him becoming a doctor. Under his father's guidance he helped tend patients that came to their home. Surely, Robert thought, he would be expected to do the same here.

The wagon was hardly unloaded and the goods moved indoors when wonderful smells of prepared food began to come from upstairs. Robert was reminded that he had not had a chance to eat the apple in his pocket.

"Your daughter cooks?" James asked with a smile.

"She does many things well," said the reverend.

Returning to the kitchen, they found the table set with bowls of stew, a plate of pickles, and bread.

"A feast!" James proclaimed.

"Well, I must not take credit for this," said Mary Margaret. "The ladies of the church provided most of this."

"And she is modest — a trait well-needed in a woman of education," her father said.

"Robert, we should wash," said James.

"You will find a bucket of water on the back porch," Mary Margaret said approvingly. "There is soap and a towel there also."

In a short time, Robert eagerly sat before his steaming bowl of stew. Mary Margaret poured coffee and joined them for the meal. He was about to take his first spoonful when he felt a gentle kick from his father. Looking up, he saw that Rev. Northland and his daughter had their heads bowed. Robert bowed his, silently expressing thanks for their new home.

After the meal, the Northlands said their goodbyes, and climbed aboard the wagon as James and Robert watched from the high porch. James put his arm around his son's shoulders.

"That Mary Margaret sure is a smart cook, isn't she?" said Robert.

"Yes," James answered, pausing before adding, "And she is smart looking."

A bit surprised by his father's comment, Robert began to laugh. Soon both of them were laughing as they stood in the doorway.

"Welcome home, son," said James.

Chapter 9

The Accident

Late into the night, well after he had gone to bed, Robert awoke at the sound of banging at the front door. He heard his father go to the door where he was met by someone with an excited deep voice.

Quietly moving down the steps from his room, Robert peered out into the sitting room. The visitor was still hidden from his view.

"James, James, ya got ta come quick. The man is in a bad way. He's barely hangin' on."

The voice was familiar. Robert stepped quietly into the room and saw Michael Shane.

"Ya got ta hurry, time's a-wastin'."

Robert raced back upstairs to dress. Whatever the problem was, it must be bad to upset Mr. Shane.

By the time Robert dressed, his father and Mr. Shane had already gone out to the wagon. Just as Robert opened the door to call to them, James turned. "There's been an accident; I don't know what I will be getting into. You should stay here, Robert."

"This is nothin' for the likes of a boy," added Michael. "Stay here, and I will bring yer father back as soon as I can."

Robert backed into the house. Outside he could hear the wagon roll away. I always help my father, he thought, frantically grabbing his cap and jacket and heading out in the darkness.

Robert ran as fast as he could along the road, following the sounds of the galloping horse and wagon. They were headed out of town. With only light from the moon, he had to be careful not to stumble on the tree roots and low worn stumps that cluttered the crude roadway.

Exhausted, Robert's pace began to slow. Suddenly he realized that he could no longer hear the wagon. He paused in the dark, listening intently. The wind made the branches of the sleeping trees rattle like the bones of a skeleton. At a distance he could hear howling— a wolf, he guessed.

Where was he?

The night suddenly seemed colder. Robert buttoned his jacket to the top and pulled his cap lower on his head. As his hand brushed his feather, he remembered that it was supposed to be good medicine, a greeting to the land.

From the trees above him came the "hoo-hoo-HOOO" of an owl. Robert felt goosebumps on his arms. "There's nothing to be afraid of," he said aloud. "There is nothing to be afraid of."

"Hoo-hoo-HOOO," came the answer.

Robert continued up the road in a quick walk. Finally he spotted the glow of lanterns in the distance. It's Father! Robert thought, running again.

As he approached the lights, Robert was startled by the sight. A wagonload of huge logs had overturned in the road. The horses had been freed, but pinned beneath the driver's seat by the weight of the piled logs was a man in great pain.

"Help me! Help me!" he kept crying out as men tried to dislodge the logs using wedges and **peavey hooks**. Kneeling beside the man, James talked quietly, trying to calm him.

"Blast ya all, move those logs," Michael shouted at the men.

"It's no use," James told him.

"What in blue blazes do ya mean, it's no use? What type a' doctor are ya?"

"I mean we will never get the logs off in time. This man is bleeding badly. If we don't get him out from under here immediately, he will bleed to death where he lies."

"What are ya sayin', James?"

"I will have to amputate his leg."

At that, the man under the wagon began to cry. "No! No!"

James sadly looked the man in the face and quietly said, "There is no other way. None."

Robert went to his father's side.

"Get the boy out of here," Michael demanded.

"No, I need his help," said James. "He has assisted before in this type of operation. Robert, get my equipment."

Robert scurried to the other wagon to retrieve the heavy bag.

"I guess ya know what yer doin'," Michael said resignedly.

"It's a common procedure — and, at this moment, necessary. I need all the light that I can get."

"Boys, bring yer lanterns an' set 'em around."

"I need them at my level, on all sides, to see without shadows. Hurry!" said James, who then instructed Robert to get his **chloroform**.

The man under the wagon moaned. "Doctor, do what ya have to, but get me from under this wagon. I don't want to die like this."

"You won't, my friend," said James.

The lanterns soon surrounded James, and Robert brought the small bottle of chloroform, wrapped in the cloth that would be used to **anesthetize** the man.

"Now the surgical alcohol." Robert handed the square glass bottle to his father, who unplugged it and poured some of the liquid over his hands.

"Robert, sanitize your hands, too."

Robert poured the cold liquid onto his hands, turning his head away to avoid the bitter smell.

"Robert, the chloroform."

Robert unplugged the smaller bottle and poured some of the liquid onto the cloth. He was careful not to lose any of the precious liquid, which turned icy cold in the air. He was also careful not to breathe any of its fumes.

Robert pressed the cloth to the man's face, and his eyes soon closed in sleep as his pain lessened.

"He is sleeping, Father."

"Then we are ready. I'll prepare a tourniquet to stop the bleeding. Take out my instruments and pour alcohol on them. Hurry, Son."

Robert opened his father's case and removed the tools of surgery. After splashing them from the square bottle, he handed them one at a time to his father, who was working quickly now.

Several times during the operation, Robert found himself wanting to look away. But knowing this was the business of a doctor, he continued to watch.

"Are you all right, Robert?" asked his father. "We are almost done here. Just a few more minutes."

The men who stood around Robert were silent. Several had turned from the scene. Michael ordered the other wagon brought closer to carry the injured man back to the doctor's house.

"Robert, get my surgical thread. And I will need bandages." Robert pulled what was needed from his father's bag.

"Should I waken him with some ammonia, Father?"

"Not in this case. He has a hard ride back with us, and it might be too much for him. We'll let him come through on his own.

"There, we've done all we can." James again rinsed his hands with alcohol. He and Robert stood out of the way as the men carefully lifted the patient onto the wagon bed.

"Careful with him, ya louts," said Michael. "James, Robert, hop aboard. And two of you others come along ta help move him when we get there."

Robert collected his father's tools and wrapped them in gauze for later cleaning. The remaining men resumed the job of righting the log wagon.

The muddy ruts of the road were beginning to freeze, making the ride to the doctor's office a hard and bumpy one. Robert noticed again how cold a night it was.

At the office, the patient was carefully placed on one of the sickroom cots. James sat with the man, lightly fanning him to help clear his system of the chloroform.

Out in the office, Robert unwrapped and washed all the tools. He soaked them one at a time in alcohol and then cleaned each with a small brush before placing them on a cloth-covered tray.

Michael had sent the other men off in the wagon but insisted on staying himself. Now he paced back and forth in the office. "Foolishness it was, unnecessary foolishness. This was all over a three-dollar bet, a three-dollar bet, mind ya.

"We had two loads of logs going to the mill tomorrow to be cut into planking for road repairs. The men were sittin' around this evening and made a wager on which wagon would get there first.

"This man, this stubborn Irishman, was determined ta win the wager, an' started out in the dark of night by himself. Of course there was nothin' for the other driver to do but to give chase.

"This one must have broken a wheel on a stump or rut or somethin'. Turned the wagon over, and here ya have him. All for a three-dollar bet!"

From the sickroom, the man could be heard moaning. Coming to the door James said, "Please, you must be quiet. The man needs rest; he is still in a very dangerous situation."

"Sorry, Doctor," Michael said. "I'll wait upstairs, if I may." Robert, who was exhausted, wished that Michael had returned to the charcoal camp with his workers.

When Robert finished sanitizing the instruments, he climbed the stairs to the kitchen. Michael sat at the table with his head down. Robert tiptoed past, hoping not to disturb him and start another conversation. Right now, he wanted nothing more than to return to his bed.

Just then there was a sharp rap at the front door. Michael's head snapped up. "What is it?" he shouted, forgetting for a moment where he was.

"I'll get it, Mister Shane," said Robert, resigned to staying up even later.

Reverend Northland and his daughter stood at the door. "We heard of the accident and are here to be of service, whether to the spirit or the body," the reverend said.

Robert stood aside to admit them, along with a gust of cold air. He took their wraps and hung them on the coat tree.

"Father is downstairs now with the man."

"Then that is where I will be," said Rev. Northland, heading for the back stairs with a brief look of disapproval as he spotted Michael.

"Ah, calico. Dash all, I'd say ya came in good time. I'm sure the doctor could use some hot food."

Mary Margaret raised her eyebrows, surprised to see the man they had so recently encountered at the dock. "All right, I will see to some food," she said, pushing past Michael with her long skirts swishing.

"Now thar is a pretty lass, won't ya say, boy? Even at this hour," Michael laughed. "I bet ya weren't expectin' ta see the likes of me again so soon. Well, you can make bets on it, I wasn't plannin' on seein' the two of you."

Michael and Robert followed Mary Margaret into the kitchen, where she donned the apron she had worn earlier. The large rough man immediately set about to try and change her mind about him.

"Ya know, missy, I'm not such a bad egg," said Michael. "I've been here in this land since it was first squatted on. I'm strong, an' I've done just about every job that this place has ta offer.

"Now I'm supervisor at the charcoal camp. Ya ever been out ta the camp, miss?"

Mary Margaret, busy at the cookstove, shook her head.

"Here, let me start that dang fire for ya. By the blue blazes, that's just the sort of thing I'm good at."

"Mister Shane, I would appreciate your help, but I would also appreciate it if you would tame the vulgar language. I find it offensive."

Michael knelt silently and worked at the stove until a small flame glowed within. He placed a few small pieces of kindling in the firebox, then closed it.

"In a moment, ma'am, ya can add some hardwood. An' please forgive my ways. I've worked with **roughnecks** in the woods for so long, I have forgotten how to act around a fine lady like yerself."

Michael lowered his head in shame. Robert could hardly believe that such a change could be brought over this big, strong man — and by such a little woman.

"That's a lesson ta be learned about ladies," Michael told Robert. "Ya should always mind yer manners and watch yer tongue, as is only proper."

Michael looked over at Mary Margaret, who was placing larger pieces of wood in the stove and doing her best to ignore him.

"Now, whar was I? Oh — the charcoal camp. I've a crew of men who chop down trees and cut the logs into four-foot pieces. Now, this is all hardwood, mind ya. None of this pine and other soft stuff will do.

"We make a mound of maybe twenty-five or thirty **cords**, and then we cover the whole 'shebang' — " Michael looked over at Mary Margaret. "Pardon me ma'am, a habit is a hard thing ta change.

"We cover the mound with dry brush and branches called lapwood. On top we pile wet leaves, and finally cover it all with earth."

"Is this all in one pile?" asked Robert.

"It's all in one pile, boy."

"But it must be a mountain. All that wood, and then to get branches and dirt and leaves on top — "

"No, no. Before we do all this, we have a huge pit that has been dug, and we pile all this into it."

Robert nodded. "Must be a really big pit."

"It is a big pit. It's a big job, to get the work done out of me crew, an' done right. Ya got ta come see it, boy, it's an amazin' sight."

Robert suddenly realized how much Michael smelled of wood smoke, which only made sense. His stubbly face, round and worn, had black specks, probably soot ground in from the hard work.

"Well, once we have finished with the piling and the covering, I set a torch to the whole she— " Michael paused. "To the whole mess." He looked at Mary Margaret for approval.

"It will burn like that?" asked Robert.

"Sure it burns, only slow. Not like missy's fire here in the stove. That's what makes charcoal. It burns for a week or so. Durin' that time, layer after layer is raked away, allowin' the air ta simmer the rest. Then we load it into wagons, or sleighs in the winter, and haul it up to the iron works.

"They use it to melt down the raw iron. A mound as big as I speak of produces about a thousand bushels, a bit more if yer careful.

"Missy, ya won't be having a wee bit of tea boiled by any chance, would ya?"

"The water will soon boil," Mary Margaret said. "Your story is interesting, Mister Shane — "

"Please call me Michael," he said eagerly.

"As I was saying, your story is interesting, Mister Shane, but as your hands tell, the work you do is dirty. Before I serve you anything at this table, I must ask you to please find the bucket on the back porch and wash yourself."

Michael cocked his head in some surprise and thought a while before responding.

"Well, missy, if that's the way you'll have it — "

"It is, Mister Shane."

"Then I'll be honoring your request." To Robert's amazement, the big man surrendered again and got up and headed for the washing bench.

"And you?" she addressed Robert. "Are you clean?"

"Yes, ma'am."

"Good. Then you may help."

At her direction, Robert began mixing ingredients for pancakes that Mary Margaret had just put into a large bowl. Meanwhile, she cut slices from a slab of bacon and put them in the skillet to fry.

As she worked at the stove, Michael pushed open the back door farther than he had to, bumping her in the backside.

"Oh, pardon me, miss — I am so sorry. I didn't hurt ya now, did I?"

"I am quite fine, thank you."

Robert, completing his job of mixing pancake batter, fought back a grin as Michael winked at him.

The cakes had just been turned in the skillet when Robert heard his father and Rev. Northland on the stairs. "I smell glorious food," said James. "It must be your daughter, as I doubt anyone else here can cook like that."

"Cakes and bacon will soon be ready — if you have an appetite to eat?" said Mary Margaret.

"I do indeed," said Robert's father. "The patient is fast asleep. I don't know if he will make the night, but I have done my best."

"You have done an excellent job, Doctor. And your bedside manner is outstanding," said the reverend as they all sat down.

"Thank you, Reverend Northland. It was my wife who really had a way with the sick. She worked by my side with every patient who visited our house, as Robert often does now.

"I have been fortunate to have such support."

"Yer wife, ya say?" blurted Michael. "Of course, the boy has got ta have a mother. I've talked so much I forgot ta ask. Whar is she now?"

Mary Margaret, already knowing the answer, was stunned by his blunt question.

"Mister Shane — "

"No, it is all right," said James. "It has been two years now since my wife and daughter were taken by cholera back in Albany. It is hard, but it is a fact.

"My sister helped me with Robert, but now that he is almost a man himself, it was time for us to make our own way."

"I'm sorry ta hear that, James. Yer wife would be happy to know what a fine job yer doin' with the boy. He's like the son I wish I had."

Their meal was filling but soon finished, and everyone was tired.

"Daughter, the sun is soon to rise," said the reverend. "I will take you home when you are ready."

Reaching into a pocket, Michael tossed a few coins onto the table. "James, this is for my man, and all yer hard work."

"No, I couldn't take that. I've only just arrived in this community, and all my needs are being met."

"I insist," said Michael. "Don't let it be said that Michael Shane doesn't take care of his own. I bet Robert would like the coins, won't ya?"

Robert, who was almost asleep in his chair, smiled and nodded.

"Boy, what would ya think about comin' ta the camp and workin' for me for a time? I have a few odd jobs around that could be done for a fair wage."

Reverend Northland lifted his eyebrows and appeared to be about to comment on Michael's offer when his daughter called from the sitting room: "Father, I am ready."

James started to rise from his chair to bid them farewell.

"No, please keep your place. I must hurry so my daughter can get some rest before she meets with her students." Reverend Northland left the kitchen, and soon the front door closed behind them.

"Well, James, what do ya think about your son working out at the camp? I'd take good care of him, and he'd be well-fed."

Though excited about the prospect, Robert could hardly lift his head.

"The charcoal camp sounds very interesting, Father."

"Yes, I am sure it does, Robert. But it's late, and I am too tired to think about such important matters. We can talk again, after we have rested."

Michael agreed and set off for his camp.

With an effort, Robert rose from his chair to climb to his room.

"Robert, I am proud of you," said James. "You were a fine assistant tonight."

Robert smiled. He knew he'd been disobedient in leaving the house and was grateful it hadn't been mentioned.

"Good night, Father."

"Good night, Son."

Chapter 10

A Perfect Gift

It seemed to Robert that he had just fallen asleep when he was awakened by sounds from downstairs. But he soon realized that the sun was already high in the sky. He dressed and went downstairs.

Working in the kitchen was a short, round woman with blond hair tightly wound in braids. She turned and gave Robert a bright, happy smile.

"*Guten tag* — good day, young man. I have heard vonderful things about you, ya? I am Karin. Your father, he works in his office below."

After greeting her in turn, Robert went down the steps to the office, arriving just as two men carried the victim of the wagon accident out the door and carefully loaded him onto the bed of a wagon.

"They are the man's brothers," his father said. "The woman in the wagon, crying, is his wife."

Michael Shane, approaching the house on foot, stopped for a few words with the woman before greeting Robert and his father at the office door.

"I asked that they leave him with us for a day or two longer, but they insist on taking him home," James said. "I can only hope he will make it."

He placed a hand on Robert's shoulder. "It is times like these that you feel more sorry for the family than for the victim."

"A woman's tears are a hard thing ta handle," Michael agreed. "She will be all right, though, even if she does become another widow of the woods. She has family about.

"Not so long ago, a whole crew of men workin' underground died. They had dug ta one side like, and were minin' ore right under a river. Men said they could sometimes hear the river against the ceiling of the dig. The whole idea scared some of them so bad they quit their jobs. Others bragged about the extra money they got for workin' in such conditions. It was minin' in a dangerous way, and it wasn't called for. But the jingle of the extra coin in their pockets made 'em do it.

"And then one day, the whole shebang let loose. The roof of the mine came cavin' in on the men. Drowned the whole lot of 'em. How the women mourned then. It was pitiful to see them standing at the shaft head, callin' to loved ones who'd been lost to the mine."

Silently, the three went up the stairs.

"Now who do we have here, workin' in yer kitchen?" said Michael, brightening at the prospect of impressing another woman.

"I'm Karin, here to help. Vould you men like some good coffee? It's fresh and hot."

James introduced Michael to Karin, who patted the table. "All of you, sit. Maybe you vould like some fresh dunkers, too? I made dem dis morning."

Robert's eyes lit up. Dunkers, his favorite!

Karin poured coffee all around and set out a big platter of dunkers.

"Now tell me, darlin'," said Michael. "With an accent like that, ya can't be Irish now, are ya?"

Karin chuckled. "You are a sly vun. I am from Finland. My whole family is from Finland, ya? But here in States now. Fine work to be found. Fine land to be farmed.

"I come here vit' my husband. He's gone four years now, God rest his soul — killed in a mining accident."

Robert swallowed hard, thinking of the sad story he had just been told.

Karin told them she had been among the first women to settle in Marquette.

"De land is so good and rich," she said. "My husband, he made me a table using vood from a packing crate for de top, and de bottom — de legs, you know — he made from a tree he cut down by our front door. De land so rich and de tree so strong, in spring dat table sprouted pretty green leaves. Darndest t'ing I ever see.

"But I have many good memories of having a husband. Maybe it's time I find a new vun, ya?" She looked at Michael with a sunny smile.

As Robert and his father exchanged grins, Michael immediately set out to show her he wasn't marriage material.

"Jumpin' Jehoshaphat, woman, I never in all me born days heard a woman as brave as ya. Comin' ta this land so early on, and from so far. Blast dang, ya even had a table with legs that sprouted. Now, isn't that a cuss of a story?"

"Oh, I like da vay you talk, Mister Michael!" she said. As he stared at her in surprise, she added, "Strong talk from a strong man, ya?"

Hastening to change the subject, Michael asked, "James, have ya had a chance, now yer head is clear, ta think about allowin' the boy ta come ta the charcoal camp an' work? I can teach him ta cut wood and pit-burn with the best of 'em. He could make a hot bed of coal as good as mine when I'm finished teachin' him."

"Michael, I don't know," said James. "My son and I have only recently been reunited after a long time apart. Besides, he is only twelve years of age."

"By twelve, I'd already worked in the mines for years and run away from me home in Cornwall. I traveled the ocean on me own and found me way here. Age has not a thing ta do with it.

"And after seein' that boy work with ya last night takin' that man's leg, I know he has a strong body and spirit. He has what it takes to face the wilds of this land, and more."

"He also has, my friend, what it takes to be a very fine doctor and help this community grow and be healthy."

"Keep talkin' like that, James, and the next thing ya know you'll be havin' the boy birthin' babies!"

Robert could feel his face warming as he looked down in embarrassment.

"Now, now. Dat is still a voman's job," said Karin. "Isn't dat right, doctor?" Everyone laughed.

"Michael, I intend for Robert to attend school here, but I can't see any harm in his learning some other skills as well, particularly with you as the teacher. After we're settled in here, if Robert still wants to, he may spend some time at your camp."

Robert's eyes lit up.

"It's a deal, though I could use the help today," said Michael. "Ya drive a hard bargain, James Friggens."

"Well, now this good company will have to excuse me," said James. "I was never able to catch up on my rest last evening, so if you don't mind, I will try to take a nap. Who knows what will happen tonight."

Michael, who was also lacking sleep, decided to make his way back to camp. Karin began bringing large washtubs into the kitchen from outside.

"Dis is good," she said. "Vit' the men out of my vay, I can do vash. Robert, do you vant to learn how to do vash?"

Caught off guard by the question, Robert shook his head "No."

"Good. Den you go outside and keep yourself busy. I don't need you under my feet."

Robert put on his coat and cap and went outside. A cold, damp wind blew steadily. He shuddered. I hope the summers aren't like this, he thought.

For lack of a better idea, Robert started walking up the road in the direction of the accident the night before. Nothing looked familiar in the daylight. But Robert decided that at least it felt like the same road, with its tree roots and worn stumps underfoot.

The wind rattled bare branches in the gray woods around him. Here and there a pine, dressed in its green coat, added a splash of color to the drab scenery. After walking for what seemed like miles, Robert began to wonder if he had gone in the wrong direction. Perhaps the accident had happened on a different road.

Just then, he heard the angry calls of a raven above. Turning to see what had caused the outburst, Robert froze. Two black bear cubs stood at the edge of the road and watched him.

Robert stood silent. He knew these bear cubs would not be far from their mother. He also knew there is no mother in the world more protective of her young than a mother bear.

The cubs soon tired of watching the motionless boy and began to play together. They swatted each other and rolled, growled, and gnawed in mock battle. At one point, both stood on their hind legs and pawed at the air in a comical dance. Robert momentarily forgot his concerns about the mother bear and laughed aloud, raising his arms to mimic the motions of the cubs. They immediately stopped their play to watch him, sniffing at the air.

With their attention back on him, Robert was reminded that the situation could quickly become a dangerous one. He was starting to back up slowly, when his boot caught in a tree root. As he tumbled backwards to the ground, the cubs squealed in fear and ran to the nearest tree. Climbing it as quickly as they could, they called out what sounded to Robert like "M-A-A-A, M-A-A-A!"

Robert picked himself up, laughing at the treed cubs. It certainly didn't take much to scare them, he thought.

Just then a full-size bear came crashing out of the undergrowth. It sniffed at the air and then stood on its hind legs, throwing its head around and pawing angrily at the sky with long claws.

Robert, wide-eyed, stood absolutely still. The bear was taller than any man, and had long yellow fangs. Robert began edging away, walking backwards, careful not to trip again. But a savage look from the huge bear took all of his courage. He turned and raced into the forest, knowing as he did that he could not outrun a bear.

Looking for a place to hide, Robert found a dead tree, rotted hollow but still standing and with an opening near the ground that looked large enough for him. He squeezed through and began working his way up inside its trunk. He pushed hard with his feet and back, scrabbling at the decayed wood with his hands.

It was awful up there, but worse below. The mother bear had pursued him and quickly found his hiding place. She raked the inside of the tree with her long claws, trying to reach him.

Robert pushed himself higher, wondering if the tree would topple with him in it. He could see light above, and at last he reached a rotted hole that let him see out.

The bear was swiping at the opening with her claws, chipping the trunk away one piece at a time as she growled in anger. Then she began digging at the roots of the tree. One way or the other, she was going to bring it down.

For the first time since he had been surprised by the bear, Robert cried out: "HELP!"

And then there was silence. The bear stopped digging and growling and turned to sniff the air. Robert looked in the same direction as the bear and saw a man dressed in **buckskin** and a fur hat, standing with his arms stretched straight toward the sky. Robert guessed he was an Indian.

The man began speaking quietly to the bear, his voice firm and steady. The bear stood erect, raising its forelegs to the same position as the man's arms.

Standing his ground fearlessly, the man continued to speak to the bear. Eventually the animal dropped to all fours and turned and lumbered toward the road and her cubs.

Astonished, Robert carefully worked his way down the tree and out the hole. As he straightened his stiff back and brushed his clothes, he looked for the man who had calmed the bear. He was gone.

"He has to be here," Robert said aloud. "Hello."

There was no answer. The man had disappeared so quickly that Robert began to wonder if he had imagined the whole strange scene.

Just then he spotted his cap on the ground. He knew it had fallen from his head as he ran, but something was wrong. The hat lay far from Robert's escape route. It was now near the place where the man had stood.

So the man was not imaginary. Robert sighed in relief. But he wished he could talk to him, ask him what he had said to the bear, and thank him for saving his life.

Robert walked over and bent to pick up his cap. The feather was missing. He looked around carefully, but it was nowhere in sight.

Had the Indian taken the feather? Robert frowned—then accepted the possibility. It was, after all, a perfect gift for someone who had saved his life.

As he walked out of the wild, wooded area, he realized that this was the way things had looked for hundreds, maybe even thousands, of years. Perhaps it wasn't so unlikely that over those years people and animals could have learned a common language. Maybe it was the people, in their rush to build towns and cut trees and mine minerals, who had forgotten the language.

As Robert reached the road that would take him home, a freezing drizzle began to fall from the gray skies above.

Chapter 11

A Clean Escape

Robert was soaked by the time he reached home, and his teeth chattered from the cold. Karin didn't seem surprised by his condition.

"De veather changed, ya? Dat is vhy I dry de clothes inside. A boy as smart as you, I thought vould know to come in out of de rain."

The kitchen looked as if there were a celebration going on. Twine was strung from wall to wall, and draped over it like banners were Robert's and his father's clothes. The combination of red underwear, blue trousers, and white shirts made it look like Independence Day.

Karin helped Robert pull off his wet wool jacket. She stretched out its sleeves and found a place for it on the clothesline.

"Dis time of year, de veather you can never tell, ya? Vun minute de sun shines bright, and de next de snow is flying.

"Vunce vhen I first arrived, I put out my vash on a nice morning, and by evening my vool **drawers** froze stiff. I pulled a leg off dem vhen I tried to free dem from de line!"

The thought of one-legged drawers made Robert laugh.

"Here, you come stand by de stove and varm up. I still have lots of hot vater from vash. You should take bath." Karen hung Robert's cap near the stove to dry.

"Oh, you lost de feather. And such a beautiful feather. Too bad."

Karin pulled out the largest of the tin washtubs and began filling it with hot water from the buckets at the back of the stove. Robert, standing by the fire, started to warm up.

"I should be all right. I don't need a bath."

"Nonsense. Hot vater is good for you. Your papa be back later. He sleep for a vhile, den go visit his patient from last night, de man from accident. Now you get ready for bath, ya."

Karin kept filling the big tub.

"I think I lost the feather when I was chased by a bear," Robert said calmly.

"Bear? Vhat bear?"

Robert told her about the encounter with the cubs and the mother bear, and then about the Indian who talked to the bear.

"Ah, Robert, you are a lucky boy. De Indian deserves the feather.

"Now you take off clothes and get into de tub."

Robert scrunched up his face in protest.

"Do you need help, like little boy?" she asked gruffly.

"No, no. I'll do it myself."

"You hurry yourself, den!" Karin left the kitchen and closed the door behind her.

Robert got out of his damp clothes and put one leg into the washtub. "OHHH, that's hot!" he complained.

Karin called from the other side of the door: "You in tub? You need help?"

"NO, I don't need help!"

A hearty chuckle came from behind the door. Slowly, Robert lowered himself into the steaming bath. "I think she is trying to cook me," he said loudly enough for Karin to hear.

After a short time he settled back in the tub, which was almost overflowing. This does feel good, he thought.

Just then Karin came back into the kitchen, ducking under the hanging clothes. "I brought you soap. You vant me to scrub your back?"

"What? No!" Robert sat up in embarrassment, his knees to his chest. "I'm fine, thank you. Just go away!"

Karin laughed at his shyness. "In my country, da family steam together like red lobsters in a pot and den go play outside in de snow. It makes dem strong and healthy. You tell me if you vant to go outside, ya?

"Sorry, Robert. Just teasing. I leave you alone now." She ducked back out the door.

Robert shook his head as he began to wash. What a funny lady. Steam together like lobsters and play in the snow? Robert was glad he lived in a place where people didn't do such things. But he had to admit the hot bath was a good idea. His last one had been two months before, at his aunt's home in Albany.

After two sharp raps at the kitchen door, Karin again swished through. "Just bringing you dry clothes and towel. Don't get up," she teased. "And be careful not to get vater on de floor. But please hurry.

I must finish here so I can go home and make a meal for my family."

She left the room, and Robert rose from the tub, dried himself, and dressed. When he was ready he called Karin, and they carefully emptied the tub, one bucket at a time, out the back door.

After putting the tub away, Karin started taking down the clothes that lined the kitchen. "If you do dis, I can cut vegetables for soup," she said.

Robert, surprised by how quickly the clothes had dried, removed them from the twine and folded them before putting them away.

"Dose shirts of your papa's, I take home to do vit' flat-iron. Leave dem by de door so I don't forget."

Just as he finished putting the clothes away Robert heard his father returning to his office downstairs. Hurrying to greet him, he found James sitting quietly at his table with his coat still on.

"Hello, Robert," he said. "I've just visited the man at his home. It's very sad. He and his poor wife have five children, and she worries about what she will do now that her husband can't work.

"His brothers all work in the mines, ten to twelve hours a day. They all have large families and their own work to to do.

"I've been trying to think of how we could help the man's family for awhile. What I really wish is that I could have done something better than take his leg."

"I can help by cutting wood, bringing water in, and things like that, Father. And it was better to take the man's leg than to have him bleed to death, wasn't it?"

"You're right. It's just that doctors sometimes have hard choices to make. You're a good son; your mother would be very proud of you."

They heard Karin's voice. "Doctor, I leave now, if dat is all right?"

"Thank you, Karin, for all your help," James called. They soon heard the outside door close upstairs.

"What do you think of Karin?" James asked. "She certainly is a hard worker, isn't she?"

"I like her. I think she and Michael should get to know each other better."

James broke into laughter and slapped his son's back as the two climbed the stairs to the kitchen. "Now that would be something."

Father and son sat down to eat the soup Karin had made for them as the wind howled outside.

"Sounds like snow wind to me," said James. "Winter comes early to these parts, just as in the mountains of New York State. I'll bet you are eager for it; I know how much you like the winter. As for myself, I could skip the season altogether."

Robert, who had been wondering whether to tell his father about his adventure that day, decided it was time to do so. James was visibly upset over the danger Robert had found himself in, but a smile broke across his face when he heard the part about the Indian.

"That's quite a story, Son. But I don't think I approve of your going into the woods by yourself."

"I'm not a little boy anymore, Father. I'm almost grown," said Robert, watching for his father's reaction.

James looked at him fondly. "I know you are, Robert. I know. But I would like having you around for a few more years."

There was a long silence between them as the wind continued to shriek outside.

"Robert, I stopped by the school today. It is just down the road and up a short path. It seems to be a very nice school, and Mary Margaret is well-respected by her pupils. I told her that tomorrow you would come and take a desk."

"But Father, I — "

"I think this will be best. I would rather you were in school than running in the woods alone."

His tone made it clear that there would be no further discussion. Robert tore open a muffin and spread jam on it. Taking a bite, he remained silent. If school was his father's wish, it must be followed.

Chapter 12

School!

Early the next morning Robert came downstairs dressed and ready, although far from eager, for school. It was still dark, and he hadn't seen the surprise that awaited him outside.

His father, who was already at work in his office, had made a pot of tea and set out some bread and preserves. Soon he joined his son at the kitchen table.

Robert, still unhappy about losing his freedom to school, ate silently.

"I have packed you a lunch of bread and cheese and an apple," James said, pointing to a cloth bundle on the work table. "It should hold you through the day.

"Son, I know you would rather explore and run free in the woods, but attending school is very important — so important that I think it should be required by law. I promise you, on your next day off, I will go with you into the woods to explore."

Robert smiled at the thought, already wondering what day that would be.

"Now, I want you to mind your manners and show Mary Margaret what a good scholar you are and what sort of a family you come from. Do you understand?"

Robert understood. He had attended school before, back in Albany after his mother died. Before that he had his lessons at home, the way many other children were taught. His mother was an educated woman and she had taught him reading, writing, and some arithmetic.

After her death his lessons had to come from a school. His father did not have to remind him of the need for education, and not just training, if he was to become a doctor.

"And make sure you bundle up well today," James continued. "Our first snow fell last night and it is heavy and wet."

A grin broke across Robert's face. No one he knew looked forward to winter as much as he did. He enjoyed **coasting**, sleigh rides, skating, and just being in the snow. He didn't even mind when the temperature dropped so low that water would freeze indoors and fires had to be tended through the night.

Grabbing his lunch, he said a quick "goodbye" and dashed for the coat tree that held his jacket and cap.

"Here, you should have these also." James handed Robert a knitted red wool scarf and matching mittens. "Your mother made these for me the fall before she died. I saved them for you. Now that you are almost a man, they should fit."

Wrapping the scarf around his neck, Robert tucked the ends into his jacket and pulled on the mittens. "They fit just fine, Father. I'll take good care of them."

Opening the door, Robert got his first glimpse of the snow. He carefully made his way down the platform steps to a world that had been transformed. Just the day before, this place had been brown and gray, looking more dead than alive. Now, as sunrise began to light the sky, everything shone and glistened and sparkled. Robert's breath formed great puffs of steam as he walked, and he was awed by the frozen beauty around him.

The path from the main road to the little school was marked by many footprints. As Robert followed their trail, he was glad he wasn't going to be the first to arrive.

It was nearly full daylight when he saw the school, a weather-worn building that looked drab against the fresh whiteness of the snow. It had double doors at the front, and a wide stairway where a dozen or more young children waited in the cold for school to start.

More than half were boys. Robert knew that many families considered education more important for boys than for girls. In many homes, the girls began helping with housework at an early age.

The older students were in the schoolyard, most of them engaged in a snowball fight. They were laughing and dodging each other's aim. It looked like fun, and Robert walked closer to introduce himself.

As he did so, a snowball swished through the air, barely missing his head before it thunked against the school building.

"Hey!" yelled Robert. Suddenly it seemed as if the entire school had stopped to take notice of the new boy. The front doors opened wide, and there stood Mary Margaret.

As Robert turned toward the door, another snowball whizzed past his head from behind him and whacked the front of the teacher's brown wool skirt. The students let out a yelp of laughter but then fell silent.

"Young man!" she said sternly.

Robert looked behind him to see who had thrown the offending ball of snow.

"Young man! You — Robert Friggens! Come here this instant."

Shocked, Robert stood wide-eyed and looked at his new teacher.

"Did you hear me? Get yourself into this school immediately. I do not put up with this type of nonsense!"

Robert's mouth hung open. How could she think he had thrown that?

"Now, march!" she insisted.

With heavy feet, Robert moved toward her up the stairs. "But, Mary Margaret, I — "

"You will address me as Miss Northland. Do you understand?"

Robert nodded. "But I didn't throw that — "

She grabbed Robert's jacket by the collar and pulled him into the school. Silently, the other children followed, removing their coats and jackets and hanging them on pegs near the door. As they entered the classroom, each took a seat on one of the benches lined up at the desks.

Robert now stood before the class, facing Miss Northland as she carefully wiped and smoothed her skirt.

"I didn't do anything, Miss Northland," he said. "I was just standing there."

"And you expect me to believe that ball of snow just flew out of nowhere? It came directly from where you were standing. I do not put up with lying in this classroom, and I will not put up with it now, even though you are new to the school.

"Will you admit the truth; or will I have to punish you for your actions?"

"But I didn't do anything."

"I hope lying is not a habit with you. Now, if you will admit you threw the snowball, I will assign you a bench. If not, you will have the corner."

Robert turned to look at the other students, hoping someone would speak up. All remained silent, but he could see they felt sorry for him — all of them, that is, except a tall boy who sat with a smirk on his face and looked coldly back at him. Robert swallowed hard.

"Well, what will it be?" asked Miss Northland.

"I didn't do it," he said.

"Fine. You will sit in the corner with the **dunce cap** on until noon." She pointed to a corner at the front of the room. There was a tall stool, and on it was a pointed hat, equally tall.

"Put the hat on, sit on the stool facing the corner, and don't let me hear a peep out of you. Do you understand?"

Robert nodded and went to the corner. The tall paper crown was so large that it slid low over his ears and fell forward on his forehead. The students started to giggle.

"There will be quiet. Lying is a serious offense." Again the room was silent, and everyone watched as Robert climbed onto the stool. If there was a worse way to start school, he couldn't think of what it would be.

Behind him he heard students reciting their ABC's. Chalk squeaked as Miss Northland wrote a series of numbers on the board. From time to time students read aloud from their books. Robert wished he were home, or even up a tree with an angry bear trying to reach him.

The time went slowly, and Robert had to adjust his hat many times. His forehead hurt and his back was stiff by the time Miss Northland rang a small bell to announce the noon recess.

"Robert, you may get down now. I hope you have learned a lesson."

Robert slid from the hard stool and straightened his back.

Pointing to an empty space beside the tall boy who Robert had decided was the snowball thrower, she said, "You will sit there, next to Mark; he's new to this school as well.

"And Mark, before you eat I want you to go to the shed and get some wood for the stove."

"Yes, ma'am," Mark said as he pulled his long legs from under the desk. Bending down, he retrieved Robert's lunch bundle from under the bench.

"Here, I found this outside. I thought it might be yours," he said, placing it on the bench space that was to be Robert's.

Robert felt worse than before. Mark wasn't so bad. Maybe it was someone else who had thrown the snowball.

All around the room, students opened tin boxes, cloth bundles, and small baskets that held their noon meals. Robert sat at his place and untied the lunch his father had packed for him. In it he found a half-eaten apple, a chunk of cheese with a big bite missing, and only the crusted edges of his bread. Mark!

Watching out the window for Mark to reach the woodshed, Robert wondered what he should do. As children chattered quietly around him, all he could think of was revenge. He took a bite from what remained of his apple and was glad that Mark apparently didn't care too much for cheese.

In the next row ahead, a boy took a pastie from his tin. "Me mother, she makes 'em so hard, ya could drop 'em down a mine hole and they wouldn't break," he said to the girls sitting across the row.

As he had hoped, the girls giggled.

"That's the way me father likes them when he takes 'em inta the mine. That's the test of a real pastie, he says." The boy took the large pastry, which looked as if it would be delicious, and rapped it hard on the desk top. Not a crumb or flake of the crust broke off. Robert had to laugh.

"Marilynn?" Miss Northland called to a small girl in the second row. "Where is Jody today?"

"She will not be comin' ta school no more."

"And why is that?" the teacher asked.

"She doesn't have shoes ta walk in snow. And ya know she lives way away, up the big hill."

"Very well," said Miss Northland.

Looking out the window, Robert could see Mark. The tall youth went to the woodshed door and opened it, then stood there for a moment. After looking around, he closed the door and ran for the woods behind the shed.

He's running away! thought Robert. Good! Maybe he thought he'd better run instead of coming back and facing me.

Pulling a shawl around her shoulders, Miss Northland went to the door to look for Mark. When she did not see him, she turned to Robert. "I would like you to please go to the shed and bring wood in for the stove. And return immediately."

The other children had finished eating and were now bundling up to play outside. Robert followed them out and headed for the woodshed.

At the edge of the schoolyard, just back from the shed, Robert could see two outhouses. In front of one, a few girls waited patiently in line. Robert hoped that if he hurried with his chore, he would have time to visit the other outhouse himself.

As he started to lift the latch on the woodshed door, Robert heard a noise in back of the building. Cautiously circling the shed, he found Mark examining a rope-like object which was unfamiliar to Robert.

Mark pushed Robert out of his way and dashed behind the pair of outhouses. Once there, he motioned for Robert to follow. Thinking this was his chance for revenge, Robert strolled casually behind the outhouses, not wanting to draw attention to himself.

To his surprise, he found that Mark had quickly climbed onto the roof of the girls' outhouse. The roof was pitched away from the school, hiding Mark from the girls' view.

Suddenly Robert understood what Mark was doing up there. The strange rope in his hand was a long string of firecrackers, with the fuse already lit.

"Don't do it!" he shouted, but Mark was already stuffing the fireworks down the air pipe atop the outhouse.

"NO!" yelled Robert, dashing to the side of the little building in hopes of warning its occupant.

From inside the little room came a racket that sounded like a hundred guns going off, one after the other. Mark dropped from the roof and ran as fast as he could for the woods.

The outhouse door flew open and a small girl, screaming in terror with her skirts stuck in the back of her drawers, ran for the school. Robert stood in amazement as the other students gathered near him.

The smoke from the firecrackers had hardly cleared when Robert felt an abrupt jerk at the collar of his jacket. Miss Northland. Nearly pulling him off his feet, she dragged him toward the school and up the steps.

"Wait! Wait — I didn't do it!" he protested.

Before him stood a teary-eyed little girl with blond curly hair, shaking and crying as she demanded, "Why did you do that to me? You beast!"

"I didn't. It was Mark! It was — "

No one was listening to Robert. It was clear that his career as a student at Miss Northland's school had come to an end in less than one day.

"I will pay a visit to your father this evening!" the teacher promised. "And I know he will not be pleased. Now leave this school immediately."

As Robert left, she slammed the doors of the school closed.

Chapter 13

New Plans

Robert wasn't sure whether to be sad or glad. He did, however, know that his father would be very upset.

As he walked up the road in the direction of home, he watched for any sign of Mark.

If I ever get my hands on him, he thought, I'll —

"What, out of school already, lad? How was Miss Mary Margaret as a teacher? I hear she can be a terror, plain an' simple!"

Robert stopped and turned as Michael caught up with him.

"What'sa matter with ya, boy? Ya look as if it were the end of the blasted world!"

Robert told him the story of his day. To his surprise, Michael laughed until he was about to turn blue.

"It sounds like Markus Simkins," he said. "His father and brothers all work in the mine, and they're a rough bunch, all right. If there is trouble at the mine, it never takes many guesses to know who is about doin' it.

"It surprises me that the youngest of 'em got sent ta school, but not that he would be up to some **shenanigans**. He probably got stuff from the mine ta make those crackers."

"You believe me?" asked Robert, glad to have met up with someone who would listen to his side of the story.

"Of course I believe ya, lad. Ya ain't tellin' me a string, are ya?"

"A string?"

"A lie. If ya be honest with me and I can trust ya like I think, I'll take yer word as one gol-blasted good man to another."

With his big hand, Michael slapped Robert on his back, almost knocking him off his feet.

"Gol' darn, boy, that's the funniest story I've heard in a long time. Come on, let's go see yer father. Maybe I can help you with this."

They found James reading in the downstairs office. With Michael's encouragement, Robert explained all that had happened.

"The Simkins boy is trouble, James, and ya know the type," Michael said when the story was finished. "Yer son, now, that's a different story."

James sat back in his chair and shook his head. He knew his son was capable of mischief, but these were not pranks he would do.

"I find it hard to believe that Mary Margaret could be so unyielding," he finally said. "She seems like a reasonable and intelligent woman."

"An' good-lookin' too, won't ya say?" added Michael.

"I get your meaning, Michael. Perhaps I have been judging a book by her — by its cover. I will have to speak with her about this."

"She said she would come to talk with you, Father."

"Fine. Perhaps she'll see things differently when she has had a chance to think about it."

"An' in the meantime, the lad and I might have a look around for the Simkins fellow," Michael suggested. "Perhaps he'll be persuaded to own up to what he did."

"Without the use of threats or force, Michael. Are we in agreement about that?" said James.

"Aye, James, if that's how you'll have it."

The search proved unsuccessful, but Robert hardly cared. His father and his friend believed him; that alone had done wonders for his mood. And the long tramp in the snow with Michael gave him a good look at Marquette and its surroundings.

Robert was describing it for his father after they had returned to his office when there came a BANG! BANG! BANG! at the door.

"Doctor? Are you there?" It was Mary Margaret.

"Come in, please," James said rather formally as he opened the door. He offered to take her coat, but she merely loosened it. She stamped the snow from her feet before crossing to the fireplace to warm herself.

"Doctor — "

"James. Please call me James."

"Very well," Mary Margaret replied, casting a stern look at Robert and Michael. Robert rose to offer her his seat at the table.

"All the fine manners in the world will not make up for your behavior today, young man," she said with a glare, then turned to his father. "I trust you have heard of the terrible commotion caused by your son at the school this day?"

"There has to have been a considerable misunderstanding," James said. "I cannot believe that my son would have anything to do with the activities I heard described."

"Well, James, perhaps that is where the problem lies. Perhaps the child is spoiled."

James, though willing to hear her out, was astonished that anyone would think so poorly of his son. What made it doubly disappointing was that the person saying these things was the most attractive woman he had seen in months.

"Surely there is something that can be done to convince you of Robert's innocence," he said.

"All the children saw the boy near the outhouse just before the explosions. And in the incident with the snowball, I myself saw the ball come from him. If he lied about one, he will lie about the other."

"The ball came from his direction. Not from his hand. You must be set straight on this," James insisted. "And Robert, in all his life, has never had exploding sticks, large or small. As a doctor, I don't consider them safe, even to celebrate Independence Day."

"You should tell your son that, sir. Not me."

Michael had heard enough. "Miss Mary, teacher or not, you need educatin' in the ways of Markus Simkins and his kind. That boy is an imp. This boy is not."

Mary Margaret got to her feet. "It is apparent that you will not come to reason over this matter," she said. "It is part of my job as a teacher to keep the children safe. I felt I could reason with you, Doctor Friggens, but I was mistaken. I must ask you to keep your son from my school this winter season, or until such time as he confesses and makes a public apology to the other children."

She turned toward the door, and James hastened to open it for her. "I can do for myself, sir," she assured him crisply as she strode out into the blowing snow.

"I've never seen the like," said James as he eased back into his chair in some shock. "I've never heard a woman speak like that before — so straightforward and strong."

"And let's not forget, wrong," said Michael.

"Yes, she is wrong in this. But you do have to admire her spunk."

"I only admire the fact she left," Michael said, and Robert nodded in agreement.

"Don't worry, Son," said James. "I am sure we can convince her of the truth. I am sure of it."

"Ya can't change the stripes on a tiger, James. But maybe this isn't as bad as it seems. Why don't ya wait for a while and just let it go?"

"Let it go? It's my son's good name being slandered."

"Just hear me out. It's clear to me, from Missy's tone, that nothin' less than her absolute certainty as regards someone else's guilt will ever get Robert off the hook with her. But, knowin' the Simkinses as I do, it's only a matter of time before Markus gets well an' truly caught at one of his pranks."

"And while we're waiting, what of Robert's education?"

"Well, surely there's some doctorin' to be learnt around here? And then, in about two weeks' time, when the snow is well set, he could go with me ta get the mail down in Green Bay."

Robert's eyes lit up.

"It's a dogsled trip and shouldn't take long; maybe ten days, maybe a bit longer. And I could use the company. I'd take care of the boy. He'd be safe and fed, and he'll come back with a few coins in his pocket and a head full of learnin' he would never know from that school of Mary Margaret's."

"That's what I am afraid of — your type of learning," James said with a chuckle. "And I can't help thinking it's more important to get this mess with the school cleared up."

"Hang that school. He'll — "

"I'll have no talk like that in my home, Michael Shane. A school has its purpose, and education is the most important thing a person can own. Once you are educated, no one — no one — can take that away from you."

"Now, James, don't get yerself all in a snit," Michael said apologetically. "I was only meanin' I could help the boy learn, too — about the great outdoors, an' such.

"Anyway, James, it sounds like you and that spunky woman need some time ta sit down and do some talkin', an' there's another reason ta get her least-favorite student out of the way for a while. That is, if ya think you can handle her." Michael laughed heartily, and James reddened a bit as he smiled.

Robert tried to get the conversation back to the dogsled trip.

"I'd very much like to go, Father," he said. "And between now and then, I could help around here with lots of things."

"An' when we get back, it will be almost time for Iron Bay to freeze," Michael added enthusiastically. "Ya like ta skate, lad?"

"Yes. Very much."

"Me too. I think I might be able ta scare ya up a pair of ice runners over in Wisconsin."

"Really?" Robert had always had to borrow the skates of other children.

"Ya know what I like best about skating?"

Robert shook his head.

"The best part is helpin' the ladies on with their skates," Michael said with a gleam in his eye.

"Michael, don't you teach my son your tricks," James said good-naturedly.

"Aw, there's nothing wrong with helping a lady lace her skates, is there, Robert?"

Robert shook his head. There wasn't anything he could think of.

"That is, unless ya try ta take a peek at the lady's ankles!" Michael burst into laughter, and so did James.

"You know, Robert, that was the very way I met your mother, helping her with her skates," the doctor said with a grin.

They heard someone enter at the upstairs door.

"Hallo! Hallo — any vun down dere?"

It was Karin.

The three climbed the stairs to the kitchen, knowing if it was Karin, there would likely be good food to follow. She stood by the stove in a big cape, with a basket under her arm.

"Oh, dere you are. Oh, and Mister Michael, too.

"I heard vhat happen. My daughter Marilynn, she tell me about it ven she get home. I think this stink good of de Simkins boy. Vhat you think, Michael?"

Michael nodded in agreement. Robert, who hadn't thought about how the story would spread, hung his head.

"Not to vorry, Robert," Karin said. "Miss Mary vill calm down and put things straight. She vill apologize. She's smart voman." Karin removed her cape and hung it on a peg.

"What ya got in yer basket? May I take a look-see?" Michael teased her.

"You keep yer mitts from basket, is for evening meal — bread und muffins und some little cakes."

"Karin, if I weren't such a miserable son of a Cornish miner, I wouldn't mind havin' ya bakin' in my cabin as my missus. Any woman, Finnish or not, that bakes like you needs ta have a man ta enjoy it."

Karin chuckled in delight, her rosy cheeks turning even redder.

After supper, Karin and Michael got ready to leave. Michael had promised to see her safely home. At the door, he turned to James.

"Is it a deal, James? Yer boy can go with me?"

James thought for a long moment.

"I suppose," he finally said.

Chapter 14

Mush!

Over the next weeks of early winter, Robert busied himself reading his father's medical books, learning the names of various herbs and their medicinal uses, chopping wood and delivering food for the family of the amputation patient.

During that time, the snow grew deeper and deeper around the Friggens house. Teams of dogs pulling sleds could often be seen and heard on the roadway.

Sometimes Robert would see Rev. Northland and his daughter in their sleigh, and Miss Northland herself stopped by a couple of times to drop off a basket of bread or a pot of stew. She spoke with James occasionally, but when she and Robert happened to cross paths, there was no more than a nod of acknowledgment between the two.

The snow drifted high. Robert had heard nothing from Michael about the trip. He worried that Michael had changed his mind, perhaps deciding after all that Robert was too young or too inexperienced.

But early one frosty morning a loud pounding came at their door, accompanied by a voice that boomed, "Come on, boy, it's time ta fetch the mail!"

Robert dashed through the sitting room and threw open the door to greet Michael Shane, who now had a full gray beard.

"Ya don't have any tea set ta boilin', do ya?" he inquired as he stamped the snow from his tall leather boots. "Here, this is for you."

He threw Robert a heavy canvas bag that spilled its contents on the floor as Robert missed the catch.

"That better not be an example of how ya catch mail bags," Michael jabbed. Robert busily examined the items on the floor. There was a heavy long wool jacket with fur lining, a fur hat with ear flaps, leather boots like Michael's that looked much too big, and six pairs of heavy woolen socks.

"All the socks are in case the boots are too big. At the mine store they only had two sizes of boots, big and small.

"That jacket will hold ya well against the cold. Mine has lasted for years, and I haven't caught me death yet."

There was also a pair of leather mittens, lined with fur. They were too large, but that was good. He could wear the ones his mother had knitted underneath.

Michael and Robert went into the kitchen, where James poured steaming cups of tea and set out a plate of dunkers.

"The goods out there is half the boy's pay," Michael said. "The rest will come in cash money when we return. Can he leave today?"

"Today? When?"

"Why, now — if he'd quit sittin' around and get himself a bag packed."

"May I, Father? May I go today, now?"

James hesitated.

"Will ya stop that, James? Ya already said 'yes.' The snow is set and deep, and I can get my sled together in less than an hour. This town has been waitin' long enough for some mail. We've not had any since the last ship near the end of October.

"We shouldn't be gone much more than ten days. Green Bay is just a run through the woods. As long as we don't hit any blizzards, we should be fine."

"And what if you do?" said James.

"Then we'll just hole up in some settler cabin along the way. We'll have plenty of food for both man and beast — smoked and dried elk, venison, and fish."

James looked at Robert, knowing such a trip would have been out of the question if his mother were alive.

"All right. Robert, get your things together."

"Ya-HOO!" Robert yelled as he darted out the kitchen door and up the stairs to his room. Michael and James laughed at the boy's excitement and began to discuss Michael's plans for the trip.

When Robert returned, he carried the canvas bag Michael had brought, bulging at the seams.

"Whoa there," said Michael. "The space on the sled is for mail, not yer toys. Let's see what ya got."

Michael emptied the bag onto the table. On top of the pile was one of James's medical journals.

"What's this? A little light readin'? The only thing that would be good for in the wilderness would be startin' a fire, boy."

James smiled as Michael took the book from the pile and set it aside.

There was also a **jaw harp**. "I've already got one," Michael commented as he tossed it out. "And all ya need is one change of clothes, as we'll be gone less than two weeks."

As Robert sorted through and repacked his things, James packed a food bag with dunkers, cheese, and bread. "We'll have ta eat those soon, or they'll freeze solid on the trail," said Michael.

Robert swallowed hard, realizing his appetite for winter weather was going to be put to the test.

"I'll be back in half an hour with the sled and team. I want ya waitin' out on the road, and wearing the clothes I brought. I'll put a pair of **snowshoes** in the sled for ya, now I know the boots fit."

Michael left the house, and James looked at Robert for a long time. "Son — "

"I know, Father. I will be all right; Michael will make sure of that. Remember, I am almost a man."

"Almost doesn't make it so. I hope I am doing the right thing by letting you go.

"Now you had better get yourself changed. Wear two sets of wool underwear, two pairs of pants, two wool shirts, and at least three pair of those socks, so those boots don't rub your feet raw."

Robert nodded and returned to his room. After stuffing himself into all the layers of clothes, he was barely able to lean over to lace the boots.

"Here, don't forget this," James said, wrapping the scarf his wife had made around Robert's neck.

"Be safe, Robert. Be smart and safe. Remember to drink plenty of water." James looked away so his son wouldn't see the concern in his eyes.

"I will, Father, but I have to get out of the house. I am so hot I think I could melt like a candle."

James smiled and handed Robert his canvas bag. "I sneaked in a small medical pamphlet, just in case you get time for some reading."

"Thank you, Father."

James hugged his son and opened the door. Slipping his hands first into his mother's mittens, then into the leather ones, Robert headed down the stairs as his father watched.

The morning sun shone bright on the fresh snow. Within minutes after he reached the road, Robert heard the barking chorus of a dog team at work.

As the sled approached, he counted five huskies in a variety of colors, with clouds of steam coming from their snouts as they galloped excitedly toward him with the sled in tow. At the rear of the sled, riding the runners, stood Michael.

"WHOA!" he called, as if to a team of horses, and the sled came to a stop. The five dogs stood nervously in line, alert for their next command.

"They're beautiful. What kind of dogs are they?" Robert asked.

"These're huskies from the far Northern Territories, strong an' tough. But ya can harness just 'bout any dog ta pull a sled. Even a hound will pull."

James, who had put his coat on and was watching from the porch, called to them: "I hope those poor animals aren't going to be pulling the likes of you too far, Michael."

"I don't often ride the sled, but I'll have ya know, these poor animals can take more cold and pull more weight than the three of us together. That one up front, the lead, is the best in the North.

"The lead has ta stay out front, keeping lines tight and the other dogs movin'. They have ta be true leaders, faster than the others and able ta do all the work."

Robert bent down to rough the fur of the lead dog with his mittens.

"Don't be doin' that, boy. They're no pets, they are workers. They need ta respect ya as the master, not love ya like a friend."

As Robert stood back from the dogs, Michael pulled a pair of snowshoes from the sled. Like the sled itself, they were made of woven leather straps on wooden frames.

"Try 'em on. Ya ever walked in a pair before?"

Robert shook his head and dropped the wide shoes in front of him. Trying carefully to keep his balance, he got one boot under the strap of a snow-shoe, then attempted to step into the other.

"Stretch out yer legs, and squat a little."

Trying to follow directions, Robert lost his balance and almost pitched forward into the snow.

"This might be a longer trip than I thought," Michael joked, and James joined in the laughter.

"Well, ya won't be needin' the shoes now. As long as we have a road, they will only get in the way. Put them in the sled, and don't forget yer bag. Some clean clothes might come in handy at Green Bay, especially if there are pretty ladies there."

"Now, Michael, none of that!" called James with a grin. Robert found a place to wedge his canvas bag in among the supplies and outgoing mail packed on the sled.

"Come, boy. You follow behind. I'll be workin' ta keep the dogs at a slow pace, but ya need to keep up. If ya fall behind runnin', I'll just have ta leave ya where ya drop."

Hoping that Michael was just teasing, Robert tried to appear confident.

"Goodbye, Father."

"Goodbye, Robert. Michael, you take good care of my son."

"That I will, James. . . . Mush! MUSH!"

The dogs leaped forward and the sled started down the road.

Chapter 15

The Great Adventure

Before leaving the roadway to begin the wilderness trail, Michael and Robert passed several large horse-drawn sleds carrying ore toward the docks.

"By the summer we should have ourselves a finished strap railway," Michael told Robert over the barks and howls of the dogs as the two of them ran behind the sled. "They plan on callin' it 'the Iron Mountain Railway.' That and the new lock at the Saulte, will speed the trip to the rest of the world. This land is growin'!"

Soon the sled and team reached the end of the cleared roadway and began following mining trails. On and on they went, with Michael stopping about once an hour to take water and let Robert catch his breath. The dogs, seeming eager to keep running, barked and fussed at each stop.

"They are like children," Michael said. "They don't want ta stay still, even when it's time ta rest. But always remember, 'run-rest-run.' That way we all keep our strength."

At one break, Michael pulled out the cheese, dunkers, and apples James had sent. It was one of the best meals Robert could remember.

The dogs, Robert noticed, never refused to eat or drink what was offered them. Their constant running demanded large amounts of energy.

Each time they stopped, Michael took the opportunity to teach Robert about working a team and sled.

"Ya have ta trust the dogs, boy. They can smell a trail when ya can't see one. Call '**gee**' or '**haw**' when ya want ta turn 'em, just like a mule or a horse. 'Whoa' will bring 'em to a stop, or it should if they're not runnin' down a rabbit or a deer."

"Why do you say 'mush' when you want them to go?" Robert asked.

"It comes from the Frenchies. They have a word 'marchez' or some such, meanin' 'march on,' same as 'go.' "

The sheer power of the dogs, all tied together on the lead line, amazed Robert. "The lead must really be strong," he said.

"Well, it takes them all ta pull. It is these boys back here, close ta the sled, that breaks us through the snow and keeps us going with their strength.

"It's 'specially hard for them on a hill. They are the last dogs over the top, with a sled at their heels. An' they have ta dig in with me and bring up the sled. That's when we all work up a sweat."

"I'm sweating right now, even in this cold," Robert commented,

"How many layers ya wearin', boy?"

"Two of everything, and three of socks."

"Ya'll need that for sleep but not for work. If ya get all sweaty, ya can catch a chill, and that's when men die in the wilderness.

"You'd better get out of some of those layers. Keep the drier clothes on. An' be quick about it."

Robert stripped to his underwear, noticing the extreme chill when the cold air hit his sweaty skin. The inner shirt and pants were damp with sweat, and he left them off as he dressed again in his outer clothing.

"Lay them across the sled so the sweat will dry out of them, and they'll keep ya warm tonight." It was one of many lessons learned that day.

As evening approached and the sun dropped behind layers of smoky clouds, the team pulled up at an old, abandoned cabin that was missing its front door but otherwise appeared sound.

"We'll spend the night here," said Michael. "It's as good a place as any. At least we'll have a roof over our heads.

"You can find some **deadfall** for a fire."

The dogs, exhausted from their day's work, were released from their harness and tied to a loose lead line. They circled together, making nests in the snow.

Michael unloaded some smoked fish from the sled and tossed a portion to each dog. Then he pulled out a tin pot and some cups made from tin cans and set about making a meal.

The fireplace in the old cabin was still in good working order, and it appeared that many other travelers had stopped at this place. As Michael noted with a laugh, the door was always open.

With the wood Robert had gathered, Michael quickly made a fire and boiled water for tea. They ate the rest of the cheese, apples, and dunkers from James. Then, thoroughly tired, they arranged their blankets on the floor near the fire and soon fell asleep.

It was late in the night when Robert awoke to the sound of a ghostly howling. The fire was nearly out, and Michael was nowhere to be seen. Just then he appeared in the doorway with a great armload of wood.

"Help me get some of this in. There are wolves about. Bring the dogs into the cabin so we can keep an eye on them.

"Wolves are smart. They will send in a female ta try an' bait the dogs out. Then they will attack and kill. Me dogs are smart, but by Jove, I wouldn't put it past 'em ta fall for that trick."

While Michael tended the fire, Robert guided the dogs into the cabin. The animals, equipped with their great, thick coats chose to lie as far from the fire as they could get.

Michael sat near the fire, a shotgun in his hand, watching out the doorway. The wind had stilled, and the only sound outside was the lonely pleading and calling of the wolves.

It took Robert a long time to get back to sleep. When he awoke, the sky was turning pink with the rising sun, and Michael was giving the dogs food and water.

"Ya slept in, boy. Get yerself some tea and a piece of **jerky**. Soon that old ball of fire will be burnin' a hole through the sky. If we keep gettin' a late start, we will never make it ta Wisconsin."

As the day progressed it seemed to Robert that he indeed might never make Wisconsin. Michael had instructed him to wear the snowshoes. But his inexperience with this equipment made his travel difficult instead of easier. In a bent-legged swagger, he plodded behind the sled as best he could, but Michael often had to slow the team to wait for him.

They were now off the worn mining trails and were following a path left by other dog sleds making their way across the cold North. The snow lay deep and heavy in the woods, and the dogs lurched into chest-deep drifts as they pulled.

The wind was sharp all day, blowing the snow into little tornadoes that Michael called **ground blizzards**. The dogs often had to sniff for the covered tracks of those that had gone before them.

This wilderness was a lonely place, and Robert could understand why Michael had wanted some company on the trip. If anything were to happen to a person alone out here, it would likely be the end. They wouldn't be found until spring — and not even then, if the wolves got to them first.

All along the trail, Michael used a hand axe to cut deep grooves into the bark of trees. **Blaze marks** he called them. "Wouldn't want ta get lost out here with that mail we'll be carrying," he said simply.

Soon Robert was helping to blaze the trail. Apart from their breaks, he and Michael exchanged few words during the day, saving their energy for the trail, which had turned harsh and hard.

By the end of the day, Robert's feet were aching and his legs and back exhausted from the snow-shoes. But the excitement of the adventure was still fresh.

That night they made their camp in a thick bank of trees to help protect them from the wind and snow. Michael used his tin pot to dig out the snow for a fire pit and laid a fire larger than was needed to keep them warm.

"I want the dogs tied by the fire this night," he said after they had eaten. "If the wolves get a sniff of us out in the open, they will try to pay a visit."

Each dog was tied to the next with a rope, and the end was tied to Michael's leg as a warning line. The dogs made comfortable nests in the snow, and Robert and Michael settled in as well. Robert chose a spot close to the fire, remembering the sound of the wolves the night before, and soon slept.

Robert hadn't slept long when an unfamiliar odor woke him. Around him, Michael and the dogs were sound asleep. But that smell. . . . As he sat up, he saw smoke coming from his blanket, and an orange glow. He was on fire!

Jumping up, he began stamping the blanket into the snow. Michael, startled awake, jerked on the dogs' rope as he sprang up, bringing the whole team up with barks and yips.

The fire was quickly extinguished. Muttering something unpleasant in Robert's direction, Michael yanked on the dogs' line to settle them again and returned to his rest with a disgusted look on his face.

It seemed as if even the dogs now realized the stupidity of the incident. Robert was sure each of them glared at him. Before lying down again, he placed a few more pieces of wood on the fire and moved his bed farther from it.

That night both the wind and the wolves were silent, but Robert recognized the cry of a lynx. No doubt perched in a nearby tree, it sounded almost like the scream of someone in distress.

When Michael nudged Robert from his sleep, the moon was full and bright.

"We need an early start. We'll run by the moon and trust the dogs.

"Care for some tea, after your 'roast of Robert' last night?"

Robert was relieved that Michael could now joke about the burned blanket.

Soon the dogs were back in harness, and another long day on the trail had begun. Robert was pleasantly surprised to find he was much better on the snowshoes. His balance was good, and his stamina had increased so much that he was hardly winded when Michael called their rest breaks.

After the sun had risen and the trail was clear, Michael noted Robert's continuing curiosity about the sled and team and asked, "Ya want ta run 'em?"

Robert eagerly stepped out of his snowshoes and up to the sled's hand grips.

"If ya want 'em ta go, ya know the call. If ya want 'em ta stop, call 'em and stand up to the foot brace an' bear down on both brakes with yer feet. The two claws there will dig inta the snow and help slow ya 'til the dogs stop runnin'.

"Don't take the sled on ice. It's too dangerous for the dogs. If ya get on overflows, the water freezes to their feet, and to the sled runners. That could kill the dogs and you.

"If ya ride, an' ya shouldn't do that too much as it tires the dogs, but if ya ride, let yer body move with the sled and lean into the turns. Push with one foot to help the sled along.

"Watch for sweepers, the low-hangin' branches. They can rip ya right off yer sled, or smash ya in the face hard enough to crack a bone. Just duck.

"All I want ya ta be seein' is the trees ahead on the trail, so's to avoid 'em, and the butts of the dogs; keep the sled right behind them.

"Trust the team. If ya don't trust yer animals, they will know it and show ya no respect. I think that lead dog has got a little timber wolf in his family tree. So let him know who the boss is.

"It's all yers now, boy."

Robert, trying to remember all he had been told, took a great breath and called out, "MUSH!" The dogs hesitated a moment at this new voice, then took off at a wild gait.

"Keep 'em in control, now," Michael hollered as he was left behind. Robert ran behind the sled as the dogs tried to pull it from his grip.

"Whoa!" he called, and the dogs slowed a bit. Before long, they grew used to his calls, and Robert was able to maintain a pace that wouldn't wear them out. The dogs pulled easily in the soft snow, following commands with a commitment to their master — Robert.

Michael followed their trail in a snowshoe trot, with a great smile of satisfaction at what his student had learned so quickly.

The trail rose gently to cross a hill, then dropped to run for a long distance beside a flat expanse of snow that Robert took to be a frozen lake.

At noon they were still along the shore and stopped next to a large boulder. Michael heaped praise on Robert for his handling of the sled and brought out a meal of smoked fish jerky — another new experience for Robert, and not nearly as bad as he'd expected.

After they had eaten, Michael and Robert walked gingerly onto the lake and soon were having great fun running and sliding near the shore.

"On our way back, this could be a good place to try out yer new skates," said Michael. Robert, who had forgotten Michael's promise to get him skates in Green Bay, liked the idea.

Michael, who had been venturing a bit farther from shore with each new slide, suddenly stopped, dead silent for a moment.

"Be still, boy!" he shouted. "Listen — ya hear that?

"Make for the shore — easy does it!"

Robert quickly made it to the snowy bank and turned to watch Michael, stepping as lightly as his size permitted. Both could hear the groaning of the ice as it weakened, and Michael had barely reached shore when it gave way behind him with a loud CRACK!

"It wasn't as solid as I thought," Michael said simply, his face pale with fear. Robert didn't have to be told of the likely outcome for anyone who went through the ice out here.

The two called the team to attention, and Michael took control of the sled. With Robert back on his snowshoes, they continued along the trail.

During the next couple of days, the weather was kind to them. The sun shone brightly in clear skies during the day, and the moon greeted them each morning.

Robert ran the sled daily, taking turns with Michael. At night, the two entertained each other with a jaw harp or swapped stories about miners, rascals, the Erie Canal, and everything else imaginable.

Hard work had a way of making time pass quickly, and Robert was surprised when Michael announced as they stopped one evening that they should reach Green Bay the next day.

Their camp that night offered little shelter. Michael built a great fire but as they wrapped in their blankets and settled to sleep in the snow, a loud chorus of howling went up. Wolves had found them again.

The dogs stood at attention, peering into the darkness. Michael loaded more logs onto the fire and stirred it to send bright sparks up into the night.

The wolves, closer now than they had been before, snarled and snapped, just back in the trees. Michael grabbed a burning branch from the fire and brandished it in the direction of the snarls. "Yah! Yah! Get yerself out of here. One day from civilization, and ya want ta be makin' a meal of us? Yah! Yah!"

He circled their camp with the flaming brand, as if staking out their territory against the wolves. Red eyes glowed in the darkness, and the dogs grew frantic as the growls and snarls got closer. Michael began piling brush and firewood in a ring around them and the dogs.

"Quick, Robert. Keep buildin' the ring. I'll get some gunpowder."

As Robert added brush and branches to the circle, Michael dug in his gun bag for a small paper packet of black powder. He sprinkled a little of the precious powder at half a dozen places around the circle they'd built, then touched his flaming brand to them. The powder took fire with a WHOOSH, driving the wolves back momentarily and soon igniting a circle of light.

Within the circle, man, boy, and dogs huddled close together, getting little sleep as the wolves continued their watch. At last the sun began to light the sky, and the siege was over.

"By Jove, I'm hankerin' for a hot meal and a soft bed tonight, without the howlin' of those devils," said Michael. "How 'bout you, son?"

Robert had to agree. Even though this trip was the most exciting thing he had ever experienced, he was worn out — and a warm feather tick on a real bed sounded just fine.

Chapter 16

The Mail

By mid-morning the dangers of the night had been left far behind. The trail showed signs of other travelers. Paths began to intersect until the trail had expanded into a roadway. Soon Robert began to see small cabins and farms.

The dogs pulled easily on the packed snow as the cabins became more frequent. At last the roadway opened into a city street, lined with shops and houses. To the east and north was a large body of water, still free of ice but covered with **whitecaps**.

"That, me boy, is Green Bay, where this place gets its name. This once was a big fur trading place. All kinds of Indians — Winnebago, Chippewa, Odawa, Menominee, Sauk — along with fur traders lived here. About everybody had a fort here — the Frenchies, the British, and then the Americans."

Robert listened closely to the history lesson. This town was not only much older than Marquette, it was much larger. The view of the bay was magnificent.

Robert watched the waves. "Does this freeze? It looks so big."

"It'd take a mighty cold winter ta freeze it clear across. It's all part of the big lake, Michigan. Lots o' water here, boy.

"Let's get the dogs bedded down and fed at the stable and check into our keep."

The town was busy with sleighs and sleds, families and businessmen. Michael, who seemed familiar with the streets, turned the dogs down an alleyway.

"Do you come to Green Bay often?" Robert asked.

"Every now and again. A mail runner needs ta go only halfway here 'cause another team brings the mail from Green Bay and leaves it hangin' in a tree. We got word the half-runner couldn't bring it for a spell. I figured we've been without mail for too long.

"People like ta stay in touch — just like the mail bag we are carryin'. When people heard we were makin' the run, they had letters written and ready for sendin' within the day."

"I probably should have written to my aunt in New York and my uncle in Detroit. They don't even know I reached the Sault," said Robert.

"Your father stuck a bundle in my hand over a week ago. Could be he tended to the family letter-writin' already."

At a stable near the end of the alley, Michael spoke to a squint-eyed man with a scruffy beard and dirty clothes, who let them put the dogs in one of the horse stalls. The dogs paced in the stall to mat the bed of straw, then drank from a water bucket and ate what was left of their provisions.

"I'll be gettin' more smoked fish and jerky before we leave in the mornin', ta feed us all," said Michael. "And speakin' of grub, let's get ourselves a room an' get ready to tie on the feed bag. While you clean up, I need to look up the postmaster here, a man by the name of Hicks.

"I'd dare say we'll leave for home shortly after first light tamorrow. An' if we have time, I'll find ya those skates."

The room Michael arranged for at the hotel was clean and warm, and after washing and changing his clothes, Robert was glad to be out of the wilderness for a time.

Their evening meal, Robert decided, was right up there with the best he had ever had. He gorged himself on ham, mashed potatoes and gravy, along with turnips, bread and pie until he could hardly move.

"Ah, food enough for a king — and all the queens of Henry the Eighth!" Michael exclaimed with satisfaction as he finally sat back in his chair, tipping it on its back legs. He opened his pocket knife and proceeded to pick his teeth, then rubbed his stomach and allowed a deep belch to escape.

"I left word for Hicks ta meet us here, an' we'll probably follow him ta the office ta get the mail. Could be there's too much of it for our sled, meanin' we take the mining mail and papers first, as there might be **cash certificates** or some such in there for the minin' business."

"What are those?" asked Robert.

"Oh, nothin' of our ta-do — just things for the minin' concerns."

"Is there money in the mail?"

"Might be. Ya never know what yer carryin', seein' as ya aren't allowed ta open it. It might be a million dollars, and it might be only a letter.

"Look at the pretty scenery." Michael changed the subject. "Dash all, I sure am glad we made ourselves presentable before we came ta supper."

Robert looked around the room. Every table was occupied, many by wealthy-looking men in suits. Here and there women were dining, too, dressed in fancier clothes than he had seen since Albany.

The woman who served them was short and blond, with wrapped braids and a sunny smile.

"Now thar's a looker," Michael said.

"I think she looks like Karin," Robert teased him back.

Michael looked at the waitress again. "Yer right, Son. Ya got a good eye for the ladies."

As they laughed together, Robert noticed the dirty, squint-eyed man from the stable sitting nearby, watching and listening to them.

He was wondering why the fellow seemed interested in them when another man, tall and thin and still in his coat and hat, walked up to their table.

"All right, Shane," said the man loudly, attracting everyone's attention. "What in blazes was Marquette thinking, trusting their valuable mail to a rascal like you?"

Michael slammed forward in his chair and quickly stood. "Hicks, ya blue-eyed bat, where ya been keepin' yerself? We been here near a week," Michael joked, "and haven't heard a thing from ya. I thought yer maker had finally called ya home."

The two men shook hands, and Michael offered an introduction.

"This here is me partner, name of Robert. He is keepin' me company on the trail, and he's a smart one with the team."

"Pleased to make your acquaintance, young man. You had best watch yourself with Cussin' Jack here, or he'll have you doing all of the work for none of the pay."

"Sit a spell with us, Hicks," said Michael.

"No, I've got to get home to the missus. But there are bags and bags of mail to go back to your neck of the woods."

"Should we go with ya now and get 'em?"

"No, we'll leave it in the office for the night. You never can tell who might try to grab it if they thought there was money to be had. When are you leaving?"

"The plans were for daybreak. Is that too early for ya ta pull yer miserable carcass from the feathers?"

"I'll be at the office at daybreak, you old cuss. Son, you take care of him, and make sure he goes to his room when he is finished here. Michael has a reputation with the ladies."

Robert laughed as Mr. Hicks started for the door.

"Wait, wait. I got ta ask ya somethin'," Michael called. He followed Mr. Hicks and the two talked quietly before Michael returned and handed Robert the room key.

"Here; I want ya to go upstairs and get settled in. I am goin' to check the dogs, and I've an errand to run. I'll be back shortly."

Michael left the dining room with Mr. Hicks.

"*Pardonez moi*," said the squint-eyed man who still sat at a nearby table. "Did I hear correctly? You are from Marquette to carry the mail? Your team, they in my stable, yes?"

Robert, who felt strangely uncomfortable, nodded.

"*Tres bien*, that is a big job for one as young as you, is it not?"

"No. I am used to it. My partner and I, we work together." Thinking some of Michael's speech might make him sound more grown-up he added, "We have a big day ta-morrow. We'll be hittin' the trail by daybreak; got ta beat the wolves back home to Marquette. So ya have to excuse me."

"*Oui, oui,*" the man nodded and smiled, showing his dirty, broken teeth.

Feeling proud of how he had dealt with the man, Robert went up to the room and settled in for some welcome sleep. He could hear the wind picking up. It wouldn't be the worst thing if a blizzard would keep them in Green Bay for a couple of days, he thought.

Robert was so tired he didn't hear Michael return to the room, and he slept soundly until just before daylight.

"Get yerself outta that soft bed, son. Thar's work ta be done."

"Where did you go last night?" Robert inquired. "It must have been late when you got back."

"I was back within an hour's time. You were snorin' so loud in here ya couldn't even hear me poundin' on the door. I had ta get the blasted manager to let me in.

"Now hurry up. Get yerself some breakfast. I've already eaten. I'm goin' to see ta the dogs and will meet you out front in twenty minutes. Don't forget, we got a town full of people waitin' for their mail."

Michael pulled on his heavy coat and hat and was out the door. Robert quickly washed and dressed and got downstairs in time to have a couple of dunkers and some coffee before Michael returned.

The sky was just brightening in the east as he left the hotel. The weather should be fine, Robert thought. But all around was evidence of the strong wind of the night before. Tree branches, sign boards from businesses, and even a large tin washtub had blown into the street.

"Come on, boy," Michael hollered over the excited noises of the team. The sled was filled with half a dozen large sacks of mail.

Michael motioned for Robert to follow and started the team out of town. Soon both of them were trotting easily behind the sled, which was heavier now and slowed the dogs.

Snow had blown over the trail in several places, and the dogs strained through drifts and around limbs and branches broken from trees. At one point they saw a horsedrawn **sledge** with a man working to remove the deadfall. As they passed, he waved.

"A man who works on the trails is worth his weight in gold, keepin' the trails open and safe for us all," said Michael. "By moving a branch or rock out of the way, he could save yer life and ya wouldn't even know it."

Chapter 17

Broken Plans

"Well, if that ain't the gol-blastedest thing ya ever seen," said Michael, bringing the team to a halt.

Robert looked ahead and saw that a huge tree had fallen across the trail.

"We'll have ta make our way around. Hold the dogs while I find us a way."

Michael put on his snowshoes and went ahead to look for a path that might take them around the tree. He returned in a few minutes.

"I found a way. It's not convenient and it won't be easy, but it will get us around."

Taking the lead dog by its harness, he began leading the team through the tangled woods. But Robert was unable to maneuver the heavy sled by himself, and soon it was caught up on a tree.

Michael helped free the sled, then said, "I'll handle this end. You take the lead; just follow my tracks.

"Ya see that break in the woods? Just on the other side is an incline that puts us back on the trail. Stop at the top; we'll have ta ease 'er down."

Soon the sled was perched at the top of the "incline," which to Robert looked more like a steep, wooded hill. The dogs stopped without a command and bunched up, uncertain.

"They don't like the look of this any more than I do," said Michael. "But we've no choice."

He tugged at the mail bags to be sure they were secure on the sled, then pulled a large coil of rope from under their supplies and tied one end of it to the frame of the sled.

"With a couple of turns of this around the base of that tree over yonder, I'll able to let the sled down gradual-like. When I'm ready, I want ya ta take the lead by the harness and walk 'em down calm an' slow."

Slinging the rest of the coil on his shoulder, he began to walk toward the tree he had selected. Just then the lead dog snapped to attention, quickly followed by the others. Too late, Robert saw the cause of their excitement. Looking up at them from halfway down the hill was a large snowshoe hare.

Robert leaped to control the lead but grabbed only air as the team plunged down the slope in pursuit of the hare. The sled went bouncing past him over the crest, already losing one of the mail bags.

In an instant the coiled rope on Michael's shoulder jerked tight, pulling him over the edge of the hill after the sled. "Whoa!" he shouted at the top of his lungs, along with a few other words that Robert had never heard before.

Robert scrambled down the hill behind it all, sliding and tumbling. The sled was now on its side and had lost most of its load, but it was still pulling Michael fast enough to bounce his shoulder against a thick tree trunk with a sickening sound.

At last the sled reached the bottom, bringing the dogs up short as it became tangled in the undergrowth. Robert made his way to where Michael lay face-down in the snow.

"Michael!" Robert struggled to roll him over, mindful of the shoulder. Michael, barely conscious, moaned in pain.

Robert retrieved some blankets from their spilled supplies, shook the snow from them, and wrapped them around Michael. Michael, the sled, the mail, the dogs — Robert's sudden responsibilities made his heart pound. He began righting the sled, wondering all the while just what he should do once he had its scattered contents gathered back together.

He was bringing the dogs to order when he saw a man in a two-horse sledge coming around the hill from the direction of Green Bay. Arms waving, Robert shouted for help.

When the man reached him, Robert wasted no time trying to explain, but simply pointed at Michael. "He's hurt; it's his left shoulder, maybe his arm, too."

"Help me get him into the sledge," the man instructed Robert, "and I'll get him to a doctor."

Michael, now conscious, struggled to his feet in pain, as Robert and the road worker helped him into the sledge.

"It's broke. The blasted thing is broke," he whispered hoarsely as he eased himself down on the bed of the sledge. "What happened to the team?"

Robert told him about the hare and assured him the dogs were all right.

"We hafta turn back," Michael said weakly.

The road worker agreed. "This will have to be set, and the sooner the better." He turned to Robert. "I cut part of the big tree enough to get by it. Can you handle the dog team and follow us in?"

"No," said Robert. Michael opened his eyes and frowned in puzzlement.

"The mail," Robert explained. "The bags are all over the place, and so are the supplies. You need help right away, and you might not be able to travel even after it's set.

"I'll get everything together, repack the sled, and then I might as well go on — "

"Blast ya, boy. You can't run the team alone!"

"No, but I'll go slow, and you and Mister Hicks can send someone out to join up with me on the trail. It makes more sense than taking the sled and mail back to Green Bay."

Michael stared long and hard at Robert. "Ya think ya can do that, find the trail an' stick ta the blaze marks? It might be nightfall by the time someone joins you."

"It's not even snowing, and there's hardly any wind," said Robert. "I came along to help, and now I can help."

Michael was silent.

"If he sticks to the trail, it won't be nothin' for someone to catch up with him in a few hours," the road worker said.

"All right, son," Michael finally agreed. "Here is yer chance.

"Be mindful, and follow the trail! I will send someone from the post office as soon as I reach town. But if ya get off the trail, no one will find ya 'til spring."

Before the roadworker turned the sledge toward town, Robert climbed onto its bed and opened Michael's coat to gently pack snow around his shoulder.

"Blast, boy, that's cold! I'll catch my death!" Michael howled.

"It will help keep the swelling down."

"I forgot, yer a doctor now," Michael joked through his pain.

"Follow the trail, hear? Keep it slow, so's a man can catch up with ya. Do nothin' foolhardy. Ya know the gun is there if ya need it, but don't ever use it unless it is ta save yer life. Ya understand? It's not a plaything, never. If anything happens ta ya, yer father will have me hide and I have no wish to lose my hide <u>and</u> a young'n I'd be proud to call a son."

"I'll be careful. You've taught me well, Michael. The team will be fine, and so will the mail."

"If a storm blows up, just stay put on the trail until someone reaches ya. And at all costs, watch out for that blasted hare!"

Robert laughed, and the two said their goodbyes. He watched as the sledge turned toward Green Bay, then began retrieving bags and baggage from the hillside.

Repacking the sled took longer than he'd expected, but at last he was back on the trail. He was proud of the responsibility Michael had given him, even though it was only for a few hours. He was in charge of the mail for the people of Marquette, and they would be grateful for what he was doing. Perhaps even Mary Margaret would be so impressed that she would apologize, he thought to himself.

As the day wore on Robert kept watching behind him for his helper from Green Bay. He began to be concerned as the gray clouds to the west turned red and orange with the sunset. He knew he was on the trail. Surely it would only be a matter of time.

Before the sun was fully set, Robert pulled the team just off the trail and into a sheltered spot in the pines. Remembering the nights with the wolves, he collected as much downed wood as he could and built a roaring fire.

After feeding the dogs and freeing them from their harnesses, he tied them together and then tied their rope to a tree. He melted snow for their water and his tea. Eating a dinner of biscuits and jerky, he watched and listened as the cold wind of the wilderness began to whistle through the darkening forest.

Where was the help from Green Bay? Robert decided it would be a good idea to get Michael's shotgun out, just in case. Handling it carefully, with the barrel always pointed at the ground, he sat with its wooden stock in the crook of his arm. His hunting experiences with his father had taught him that you could not be too careful when handling a gun.

Soon blackness surrounded his camp. The dogs had already made their nests in the snow; it was time to rest. When he awoke, surely, Michael's replacement would be there.

Nestling close to the fire — but not too close — Robert lay down. He had just closed his eyes when he heard a low, moaning howl.

Robert sat up and listened carefully. It was in the distance, but it was a wolf. He piled more wood on the fire, then sat fully awake. He listened and tried to see into the forest, at the same time fighting the fear that set in at darkness.

It wasn't long before he heard something. It was something walking, slowly, not like the scurrying of wolves. And it was careful where it walked, not like a bear or lynx. More like a man.

The dogs raised their heads and cocked their ears forward, a sure sign that the sounds were not in Robert's imagination. Holding the shotgun, he shifted his position to face in the direction of the noises.

"*Bon soir!*" came a voice from the blackness. Robert felt a rush of relief. It must be the man sent by Michael.

"Yes! I'm here," he called, standing up and bringing the dogs to their feet as well.

"I see you there," said the voice. "And I know what you are carrying. If you simply walk away from your camp, I will give you no trouble, *mon ami.*"

Robert didn't answer. What did he mean, walk away?

"Did you hear me, there? I will give you no trouble. I know you have the mail and the certificates for the mines."

The voice sounded very like the squint-eyed man from the stable — but that was not someone Michael and Mr. Hicks would have trusted, Robert thought.

"Are you from the post office? Did Michael send you?" he called.

A low, unpleasant laugh came from the woods. "You might say that, *monsieur*. Your friend, I saw him return to town. I also saw the one he sent. Now that one will not be coming." He laughed again.

"I mean you no harm, *mon ami*, but I have come for those mail bags, and I will have them by the time the sun rises. The night is long, no?"

Robert raised the shotgun and pointed it into the woods. "Get out of here — go on!" he shouted. "I have a gun!"

"That is good, little boy. I will wait, and when you sleep I will be there!"

Robert stood listening for a time, but the man said nothing further. The dogs, sensing danger, paced and pulled at their rope. Robert tugged back on it to reassure them, then sat close to the fire.

He had a gun; maybe the man did not. If he could just get through this night, the weapon might give him enough protection to race back to Green Bay.

As he sat, his eyes began to sting for want of sleep. At times sounds of movement in the woods brought him back to full alertness. The howling of wolves could be heard again, but now louder and closer. Robert fed the fire, thinking more than once that he saw glowing eyes among the trees.

Were they man or beasts? In his situation, did it make much difference? Robert wished for the company of Michael or his father. But, wisely or not, he had taken on this job. Now he would have to see it through. He was almost a man who had learned much about surviving in the wilderness, and he had the gun. . . . Against his will, Robert's eyes slowly closed.

His sleep was deep but interrupted with a shock as the tall figure of a man jerked him to his feet with a hand across his mouth. Robert reached around frantically for the gun but could not find it.

"Be silent. We must go!" whispered the stranger.

Pulling away, Robert was able to see the man more clearly in the firelight. He appeared to be an Indian and was wearing a fur hat and bearskin coat.

"We must go — now. I am here to help," he said in a low voice.

"Where'd you come from? Who are you?"

"You do not know?" The man put his mittened hands in the air to mimic a bear's dance, then took off his hat to show Robert the hawk feather stuck in it.

"The man from the woods, with the bear!" said Robert, astonished. "You're not the one who wants to steal the mail?"

Shaking his head, the man said, "Would I save you once, just to take your spirit now? Our fates are joined together like the roots of a great tree."

He picked up Michael's gun and unloaded it. "This power is no good; only this power is good medicine," he said, patting his chest and head. "Mind and spirit put us on the right path. Let us go."

Harnessing the dogs, the man spoke softly to them, and for the first time since Robert had been on the trail they didn't begin their work with a chorus of barks and yelps.

Chapter 18

Flight

In the darkness they silently returned to the trail, continuing in the direction Robert had been heading. The Indian, on snowshoes, led the dogs. Robert guided the sled, watching behind when he could for the danger he knew was there.

After several miles they stopped as the first glimmer of pink light began to show in the eastern sky. The man unwrapped dried venison and berries from a pouch, sharing it with Robert and the dogs.

From another pouch he brought a pipe and pushed tobacco into it. Without lighting it, he raised it in both hands as Robert watched.

"It is to give thanks for a new day and to those who watch over us," the Indian explained. "We will smoke this together when we are safe."

"I couldn't smoke that," Robert said with a look of distaste.

"You not smoke with me? This is important pipe, filled with **kinnic-kinic**. If you not smoke, then I cannot trust you."

He brought the pipe to his mouth and pulled at it as if it were lit. "Here, you smoke now, with no flame."

Thinking this strange but not seeing any harm, Robert took the pipe and sucked on the stem. It had a sweet wild taste.

"I am Robert. What is your name?"

The man smiled. "Osawa Anang. Yellow Star."

"O-sa-wa — "

"Osawa Anang — Yellow Star," he repeated, pointing up to the sky.

"Osawa Anang. I like that," Robert said with a smile. "How did you find me? Do you have some sort of magic?"

"Not magic. I was in Green Bay when I saw your friend brought in, hurt. I heard him asking for someone to be sent to help you. I also see Squint Eyes. He offered to help, but your friend say 'no.' Another man was sent, but I see Squint Eyes follow.

"After he was out of sight, I follow both. Not far from town, I found blood in snow, and first man's snowshoes, broken against tree. Only one trail went on — Squint Eyes'.

"I trail Squint Eyes until dark came, then stopped until wolves began calling. Squint Eyes too lazy to start a fire, so he was up in tree, with wolves circling underneath. I went around to reach your camp.

"I heard the wolves snapping and snarling," said Robert. "I thought they were fighting over which ones would eat me. I was trying to stay awake — "

A shot rang out behind them. Not only was Squint Eyes on their trail, but he had a gun.

The dogs, startled, barked and tugged at their harness. Quickly, Robert and Yellow Star brought the team to attention and started the animals running hard across the snow.

On and on they traveled, not daring to stop to rest the dogs. Once they heard another shot. Sometimes, when crossing a low hill, they could make out the figure behind them. The man wore a large pack, and he seemed a bit awkward and clumsy on his snowshoes. Was it possible they could get away from him, even with a loaded sled?

At midday Robert and Yellow Star found shelter behind a ridge and took the chance of stopping for a short time to feed and water the exhausted team.

Robert was sure, even over the howl of the wind, that he could hear wolves.

"Listen," he said.

Yellow Star stood silently, lifting his head toward the sky as if sniffing the air, and nodded. "We find a strange thing this day," he finally said. "Wolves are following the trail of the evil that follows us. We must go!"

Soon they were back on the trail, following the blaze marks left by Michael and others. They traveled as fast as possible and rested only briefly.

Finally the long and grueling day turned into night. Yellow Star directed the team off the trail along an outcropping of rock, then stopped at the entrance of a cave.

"How did you know this was here? Have you been here before?" Robert asked.

"When you live with nature, you must become a son of the Earth. Tonight we are like bears. Listen to the nature inside you, and use the strength of the bear.

"There will be no fire tonight," he instructed as he pulled the mail bags from the sled. Robert brought the dogs into the safety of the cave. Yellow

Star gathered cedar boughs in the darkness and used them to brush out their tracks and then to cover the cave's opening. Robert, remembering that the mail had been double-bagged, used the outer bags to line the stone floor.

"Do you think he will find us here?" he asked.

"It would be easier for him to capture the wind. We are safe; rest now."

Huddled in the blackness, they shared the warmth of the dogs and stole a few hours of much-needed sleep.

Before daybreak they again ate a cold meal and returned to the trail, finding no sign that Squint Eyes had passed them in the night. Snow was falling now, and the wind blew dark gray clouds across the sky with great speed.

They traveled hard all morning, with no sign of their pursuer. Lacking the time to melt snow, Robert broke the ice on ponds or streams to fetch water for the dogs when they paused.

By late afternoon, the snow had stopped and the wind had eased. As they came to a boulder next to a broad, flat expanse of snow, Robert recognized the place where he and Michael had played on the ice just a few days before. Yellow Star pointed out the boundaries of the lake, and Robert shared his story about the cracking ice.

"This was just a few days past?" the Indian questioned.

"Yes."

"Maybe we can set a trap. Quickly — take two outer sacks from mail and fill them with leaves if you can find them — or loose snow."

Robert did as he was told. Yellow Star cut two short pieces of rope and attached them to the trailing tips of his snowshoes, which he then slung on his back.

"Stay on the trail," he told Robert. "There can be only one set of tracks. If anything happens to me, do not try to save me. Go on to Marquette."

Dragging a mail sack on each side of him, Yellow Star crossed the shore and began to walk out on the snow-covered ice. Robert, not understanding his intention but knowing the danger, shouted after him: "No!"

Yellow Star didn't look back. Cautiously creeping and listening, he went straight out, continuing even after Robert began to hear the ice groan.

Finally Yellow Star bent over and slid the bags ahead of him toward the thin ice in the middle of the lake. He walked gingerly on toward them for a few more paces, then turned and put on his snowshoes. But he wore them backwards, using the lengths of rope to help him lift their points as he walked back to shore. As he walked, he carefully covered each of his earlier footprints, leaving a snowshoe trail that appeared to head out onto the ice without returning.

"If the man still follows, he knows we are two. But he will believe we have parted here. In his greed, he may go after the bags without removing his pack, and the ice is close to breaking. It is a mean trick, but not meaner than this man."

To complete the trick, Yellow Star rode on top of the sled for a distance as Robert drove the team. Then the two of them moved the sled and team off the trail and into a thicket, sweeping away the tracks of their turnoff with cedar boughs.

Yellow Star pulled the dogs down and spoke softly to quiet them. They had barely hidden when the man came into view, running as best he could on his snowshoes. He looked behind him frequently, fearful that wolves still stalked him. Within a few minutes the man reached the point where Yellow Star's trail diverged from that of the sled. As he stopped, Robert could see him clearly. It was the man who had asked him so many questions about the mail. "Squint Eyes," as the Indian called him.

Looking all around, Squint Eyes caught sight of the mail bags lying offshore. But instead of rushing to them, he pulled a shotgun from his pack.

"He smells a trap. But his greed will be his end," said Yellow Star.

Robert watched as the man slowly approached the shore, following the snowshoe tracks and trying to see where they went beyond the mail sacks. "The rat takes the bait," he said quietly.

Stowing the gun in his pack once again, Squint Eyes made his way farther onto the ice, moving with more confidence toward his prize. He was looking only at the mail sacks when a single large black wolf came loping up the trail behind him and stopped just at the shoreline, watching him.

Then they heard a long CRA-A-A-CK — louder than the one that had driven Robert and Michael from this same lake. It was followed by several lesser cracks, then a series of rumbles. The ice was breaking into large sections, with open water between them.

Squint Eyes, suddenly realizing that the weight of his pack could take him to his death, slipped out of it and flung it as far from him as he could. Forgetting the mail bags, he began to make his way toward shore, jumping from floe to floe.

He had nearly reached solid ground when he heard a snarl and saw the wolf waiting in his path. Squint Eyes turned aside, seeking another way to safety. The wolf trotted along the shore to head him off.

Squint Eyes swung in the opposite direction, jumping to another floe, but the wolf easily countered each move he made not letting the man ashore.

Robert watched silently until Yellow Star said, "It is time. What happens now is not for us to decide." Robert was startled by the comment, but followed the Indian's lead.

Quietly taking the sled and team out of hiding, they pushed on along the trail. Both the wind and snow had picked up again, making travel difficult.

Finally the darkness and blowing snow forced them to stop. Robert guessed it was near midnight, and that they may have covered two days' worth of trail in one. Yellow Star found a shelter among the trees and showed Robert how to dig a snow cave just large enough to hold him.

The Indian also dug a fire pit, but the howling wind made it very difficult to start a fire. "I need something dry," he said. "Let me have some of the mail; now it can help us."

Robert was reluctant to lose a single piece of mail, but he remembered the medical pamphlet his father had added to his bag and quickly dug it out. Michael had been right — his reading material would be good for starting a fire.

Soon Yellow Star had a roaring blaze going, and the two of them managed to prepare a hot meal in the blowing cold.

After they had eaten and the dogs had been tended, Robert followed Yellow Star's advice and lined his little cave with spruce branches. He crawled in and he found the snow nest surprisingly warm even though the blizzard raged most of the night.

After a sound sleep, Robert awoke to find the entry to his cave entirely closed by the night's snowfall. Breaking through into the morning light, he was glad to learn the blizzard was over and the wind stilled. At least a foot of new snow lay over everything, including the dogs' nests.

Following their safety line, Robert uncovered the dogs. They got to their feet, shook the snow from their fur, and made it plain they were hungry.

Surprised that he was up before Yellow Star, Robert built a small fire and fed and watered the dogs. But there was still no sign of the Indian. Robert was brushing the snow from the sled when he found the hawk feather attached to the drawstring of a mail sack.

Startled, Robert ran through the deep snow to Yellow Star's shelter and scooped away the snow covering its entrance. The snow cave was empty — and looked as if it had not been slept in.

Robert looked around for tracks but found none. For the second time the Indian had saved him and vanished. But this time Robert had the feather. Perhaps it meant that he was close to home — and safety.

Chapter 19

The Homecoming

Tucking the delicate feather into his fur hat, Robert prepared his morning meal and then began breaking camp.

Except for being slowed by the powdery new snow, he had a perfect day for running a dogsled. Even when breaks in the forest made the blaze marks far apart, the dogs had no trouble holding the scent of the trail. Although he was eager to reach home, Robert took care not to overwork the dogs in the deep snow.

By late afternoon Robert's excitement grew as he found the first signs of the miners' trails. He was nearing Marquette! But it was full starry darkness before he finally spied his home. Outside sat a horse and sleigh. Mary Margaret?

Robert brought the dogs to the side of the house. As much as he wanted to burst through the door and be welcomed and fed, he knew his first responsibility was to the dogs. He divided the last of their food, and the dogs barked in excitement.

"Who is out there? Is someone there?" It was James, calling from the doorway above. Robert walked to the foot of the stairs.

"It's only me, Father."

"It's Robert! Robert is home!" James called to his guest, then dashed down the stairs to throw his arms around his son. "You're home! And you're safe!

"Come in. Let's get out of this cold."

"I must get water for the dogs first, and bring the mail bags in — "

"Then I will help!"

James ran up the stairs and returned with a bucket of water for the dogs as Robert began pulling mail sacks from the sled. Mary Margaret now stood at the door, holding an oil lamp.

"Take them in through my office door. Mary Margaret, please open the door below."

Finally, with all the bags inside and the dogs settled for the night, Robert made his way upstairs to the warm and cheery kitchen. It seemed as if he had been gone forever.

Mary Margaret busily prepared food for the traveler while his father peppered him with questions.

Robert was silent, not knowing where to begin. He pulled off his heavy fur mittens, then his mother's knitted ones, then his coat.

"You have another feather," his father observed as he pulled off his hat and dropped into a chair.

"It's the same one, Father," he began. . . .

Mary Margaret brought hot tea and venison stew and joined them at the table to hear the story. Before long the eyes of both adults were wide with disbelief and shock. By the time he had finished his food and his story, Robert could barely keep his eyes open. He climbed the stairs to his room and tumbled exhausted into his bed.

He awoke in the morning to the barking of dogs. Downstairs, someone banged loudly at the door and shouted. "James! Robert? Blast, will someone answer this door?"

It was Michael. But how could that be? Robert bounded down the stairs and pulled open the door. It was indeed Michael. Another man stood with him.

"Well, do we have ta stand out here forever?"

In disbelief, Robert opened the door wide, and the men entered the sitting room. They stamped the snow from their feet, and Michael used his right hand to open his coat. His left arm was in a sling.

Robert's father joined the group, and the other man was introduced as Mr. Sorenson.

"See what yer boy done ta me, James?" Michael joked.

"If he hadn't made it back home safely, I dread to think what I would have done to you," James replied.

"Ya made it back safe, son!" Michael went on. "Who was with ya?"

James interrupted. "Let's put some coffee on." He led the way into the kitchen, where Michael told his story.

Even before going to the doctor's office in Green Bay, he said, he'd arranged with Mr. Hicks to send a man out to join Robert. But it wasn't long after his broken bone was set that the man returned, bloody and bruised, without his snowshoes.

"From his story, it sounded like that Frenchy from the stable had seen a chance ta make some money. Right then I knew I had ta go. I hired two men to come with me, with a sled an' team.

"We found your trail and the Frenchy's all right, but with the tracks of someone else. Who'd ya have with ya? And how in blazes did you manage ta get that fella out on the ice?"

"Did you find Squint Eyes? Was he alive? That skunk!"

"Robert, don't talk like that," said James.

"Father, that's the man I told you about. He'd have killed us if he had a chance. I know he would."

"But who is 'us'?" Michael questioned.

Robert told his story about Yellow Star and his help, and then Michael continued.

"All I know is, we came to the lake and there floatin' on an ice cake was this Squint Eyes, and the darndest thing — on shore sat the biggest black wolf I've ever seen in all my born days, just lickin' his chops, just anticipatin' a meal.

"That wolf skulked into the woods when he saw us, but when we brought ol' Squint Eyes ashore, it commenced such a howling like I never heard — worse than the night before we made it ta Green Bay, remember?

"Squint Eyes, even though he was frozen ta the bone, pushed one of my men over and managed ta grab his revolver. But instead of takin' aim at any of us, he started shootin' at that wolf, until he'd emptied the gun. And that wolf stood there, just back in the woods, starin' him down. I never saw the like of it.

"After the bullets were gone he threw that revolver, hard as he could, at the wolf. Still it just looked at him. Finally it walked off into the brush.

"I think, out on the ice cake, that Frenchy plain lost his mind. We tied his hands, though he was peaceable enough, just mumblin' about the wolf, and the other man with me walked him back to Green Bay ta face the law."

"Good!" Robert exclaimed.

At the back entry came a soft tap, and the door was pushed slowly open. It was Karin.

"Oooh, you are back, Robert. Good; everyone be excited to finally get de mail." She gave a big smile to Michael and then noted the sling.

"Oh, you poor t'ing! Vhat has happened to you?" She rushed to Michael's side and carefully hugged him. "You should haf someone to look after you, ya?"

Michael was speechless for a change, and James and Robert exchanged grins.

At the front door there was another knock, and James went to answer as Karin busied herself with preparations for a large meal.

Through the kitchen doorway came Mary Margaret and her father.

"There you are, young man, and Mister Shane," said Rev. Northland. "We are truly glad you have arrived. James, with your permission I will unhook the door downstairs, as men are here for the mail."

He disappeared down the stairway.

"Miss Mary, did you tell dis boy about Markus?" Karin asked. "Did you apologize to de boy?"

"Well, Karin, there really hasn't been time," Mary Margaret said, swallowing hard.

"It appears, Robert, that I do owe you an apology for the incident with the firecrackers — "

"Ya, and de snowball, too," Karin put in.

"Well, yes, and the snowball too. It appears that Mark — you know, the tall boy?"

Robert nodded.

"Well, he was caught dropping firecrackers into the ladies' outhouse at church! When confronted, he told of doing the same thing at school. It was odd, how proud he seemed of his behavior."

"Don't forget de snowball."

"Yes. Well, it appears that Marilynn — "

"Ya, my Marilynn," Karin interrupted. "She see dat Markus t'row it, but she vas afraid. She is only little-bitty girl, an' afraid of Markus. But vhen he vas caught at de church, she tell everyt'ing."

"That is why I truly owe you an apology," Mary Margaret said to Robert. "I have already told everyone the facts at the church, and I will make this right when school resumes in the spring.

"I was raised to detest lying, and when I thought I had caught you doing so, I was blinded to everything else. I am sorry, and I hope you will accept my apology."

"Well, I don't know, blast it, Missy," said Michael.

"No, Michael, I do accept it," Robert said. Maybe Mary Margaret wasn't that bad after all, he thought. And after what he had been through, the incident at school didn't seem as important.

"Well, it sounds like a lot has been going on here since we left, eh boy?" Michael said, addressing the remark to Robert but looking at his father.

James, standing beside Mary Margaret, looked at her and smiled.

"Well, I got ta get my dogs home and then give this shoulder some rest," said Michael.

"Robert, ya were the best company I could have picked ta be with on the trail. By the way," he said to the man from Wisconsin, "where's that bag?"

Mr. Sorenson brought out a small canvas bag and placed it on the table. "I believe Mister Shane said these were for you," he said with a smile.

Robert quickly opened the bag and pulled out a pair of shiny ice skates.

"You remembered!"

"Of course I remembered. I made ya a promise, didn't I?

"Now, don't you forget, son. . . ."

• • •

"Son! Robert! You know, there are lots of things I can tell ya, if you just stay awake. You hear me?"

Robert straightened his stiff back and stretched, realizing he had fallen asleep in front of Mr. Friggens' fireplace. And what a dream he had had!

"Have a look at this." Mr. Friggens held an old revolver toward him by its barrel. "But don't go tellin' your mother about it. You know how it can be with women.

"This must be a hundred years old, maybe older. I found it one day on a huntin' trip. I'd sure like to know the story behind this thing."

Robert stared at the gun, thinking back to Squint Eyes and the wolf, and shook his head. It couldn't be. It just couldn't.

"You'd better be gettin' on home now, Robert. There's quite a blizzard out there.

"But I've plenty more stories to tell you. Come on back tomorrow, if you want. My walk will need shovelin', and I'll tell ya about a wise old medicine man by the name of Yellow Star."

As he bundled up at the door, Robert noticed the old-fashioned skates again. Next time he'd want to ask Mr. Friggens about those, for sure.

Robert made his way through the blowing snow and across the driveway. He had stopped to check Thor who was happily nested in his dog house, when something in the snow caught his attention. A hawk feather stuck in a drift, holding firmly against the strong wind.

Robert stood in the cold night, holding the feather. Good medicine, he smiled as he thought about his eventful evening.

Before he had stamped off all the snow on his boots or greeted his mother, Robert made his way to the shelves that lined the kitchen walls. There between two of his father's hawk carvings, he gave the feather a place of honor.

anesthetize. To give someone a drug or gas which makes them lose feeling or consciousness.

anemia. Low iron count in the blood, making one appear pale.

anti-fogmatic. Alcoholic drink.

asthma. A disorder causing difficulty in breathing.

blaze marks. Cuts or scrapes on trees that have been made to mark a trail.

bloom. A lump of iron produced by melting iron ore in a blast furnace.

boardinghouse. A house where travelers can rent a room and buy meals.

boundary lines. Formal, imaginary lines created by a surveyor to divide land into counties, townships and villages.

buckskin. Leather made from skins of deer.

Burt, William. The surveyor who found iron in the Upper Peninsula.

calico. A fabric printed with a pattern on one side. Michael uses the term to refer to women (who wore skirts of calico).

canal boat. Narrow boat that traveled along a canal. These boats were towed by horses or mules that walked beside the canal.

cap lamp. A lamp (oil or candle) that attached to a miner's hat.

carpetbag. Suitcase made from a piece of carpet.

cash certificates. Certificates representing amounts of money designated by the lender.

catawampitously. One of Michael's special words that means at a particular angle — or not quite where the sails should be so that the wind could jerk and tear them. The word comes from catawampus, or out of line.

charcoal camp. A working camp in the woods which made charcoal for use in blast furnaces used by the iron industry.

chloroform. A liquid which was used by doctors in the mid-1800s as an anesthetic. The vapors of chloroform were breathed in by the patient to produce unconsciousness.

cholera. Epidemic illness much like a flu and caused by unsanitary conditions.

cipher. To solve arithmetic problems.

Cleveland. A mine owned by the Cleveland-Cliffs Iron Company.

coasting. Sledding.

colic. Pain in the abdomen common to infants.

cords. A unit of wood measuring eight feet long, four feet high, and four feet wide.

corduroy. A surface made of logs.

cross lots. Moving from one place to another.

cupping. The use of small glass cups to form a vacuum on the skin and bring blood to the surface. Early doctors believed that taking blood from a patient's body would reduce fevers.

dandy. City folk, one not knowing the ways of the country.

deadfall. Dead or fallen tree branches.

drawers. Underwear with long legs.

dunce cap. A tall, pointed cap intended to mock the wearer.

dunkers. Doughnuts.

Erie Canal. A canal that ran from Albany to Buffalo, New York. Many settlers traveled it to the west.

feather tick. Mattress stuffed with feathers.

gee, haw. Expressions used in driving animals. Gee means turn to the right; haw means turn to the left.

ground blizzards. Snow which is swept up from the ground and blown around by the wind.

hard spirits. Alcoholic beverages.

herb women. Women that made use of herbs and plants to treat illnesses.

icehouse. A building for storing ice before there were refrigerators or freezers.

innards. Intestines.

jaw harp. Simple mouth instrument that was popular with fur traders.

jerky. Strips of meat which have been preserved by drying in the sun.

King Tutankhamen. Ancient Egyptian King known for building a kingdom of great wealth and culture.

kinnic-kinic. A mixture of bark, dried leaves, and sometimes tobacco smoked by Indians and settlers.

letter of credit and reference. A letter stating that Robert's bills would be paid from his father's account at a particular bank.

maple sugar. A sugar produced by boiling down maple syrup.

Marquette, Jacques. A priest and explorer who established several missions in the Great Lakes area.

meteorites. Stony metallic masses that fall to earth from outer space.

Métis. One who is part French and part Indian.

oral history. Spoken rather than written stories of one's history.

pack rat. Someone who collects and keeps many different things.

pasties. A pastry filled with meat and vegetables.

peavey hooks. Iron hooks on long wooden handles used especially to move logs.

portaging. To carry something overland from one water to another.

rag carpets. A carpet made by the weaving together of rag pieces.

roughnecks. People with rough, coarse manners.

ruffian. A bully or a troublemaker.

Sault de Sainte Marie. A French name meaning rapids of the St. Mary's (river). Today we call the area the Soo, which sounds like the French "sault".

schooner. A sailing boat with at least two masts.

scores. A great many.

shenanigans. Actions that cause trouble.

sled dog. A dog trained to work with a team of dogs to pull a sled.

sledge. A vehicle on runners and often drawn by animals.

snowshoes. A set of frames with rawhide strings that look much like tennis racquets. Snowshoes are attached to one's boots and keep the user from sinking deep in the snow.

solar compass. A compass which takes its readings from the direction of the sun, as opposed to one with a magnetized needle that is drawn to the magnetic north.

stipend. A periodic payment or salary.

strap railway. An early railway with wooden rails. Thin strips of iron were strapped to the tops of the rails to make them more durable.

strikers. Matchsticks.

surveyor. One who determines the exact boundaries of a piece of land by using measurements and mathematical formulas.

tack. The direction a boat travels in relation to the wind.

Three Sisters of the Lake. A series of three large waves, each one stronger than the next.

thunderpots. Containers used as toilets.

Toledo War. Also called the "Bloodless War". It was fought over the boundary between Ohio and Michigan. The narrow strip of land included the town of Toledo. The United States Congress settled the problem by giving the strip to Ohio and the western U.P. to Michigan.

U.P. Abbreviation for Upper Peninsula of Michigan.

venison. Meat from deer.

vials. A small glass containers for holding liquids.

whisks. Small bunches of herbs or grasses.

whitecaps. Waves with white crests.

wrathy. Angry or strong.

CLINTON-MACOMB PUBLIC LIBRARY
SOUTH

CMPL
WITHDRAWN